SHOWDOWN!

"When I drop this handkerchief, you both go for your guns," said the old man, and he raised the handkerchief in his hand.

"Sure," said Sammy. "I'm ready whenever Washburn is. But you better wait till he gets over being so nervous. You see how he's shaking, partner."

"I'll blow you in two!" cried the big man.

But Sammy did not even look toward the fluttering handkerchief. No use for him to match his speed against the lightning skill of the outlaw. Instead, he leaned back and calmly watched Washburn.

"Take a last look around . . . that blue sky you'll never see again, Washburn."

"You little rat!"

"Some rats kill snakes."

"You, there . . . drop that handkerchief! Get this over with!"

"Quickly!" said Sammy, and marveled to find that he could be smiling as he spoke. "My friend Washburn is losing his nerve rapidly . . . rapidly."

With an angry outburst Maurie Washburn reached for his gun. From the corner of his eye Sammy Green saw that the handkerchief had not dropped, but, as the big man reached and whipped out his weapon, Sammy followed suit.

Other *Leisure* books by Max Brand:
TWO SIXES
SIXTEEN IN NOME
THE ABANDONED OUTLAW
SLUMBER MOUNTAIN
THE LIGHTNING WARRIOR
OUTLAWS ALL
THE ONE-WAY TRAIL
THE BELLS OF SAN CARLOS
THE SACKING OF EL DORADO
THE DESERT PILOT/VALLEY OF JEWELS
THE RETURN OF FREE RANGE LANNING
FREE RANGE LANNING
WOODEN GUNS
KING CHARLIE
RED DEVIL OF THE RANGE
PRIDE OF TYSON
THE OUTLAW TAMER
BULL HUNTER'S ROMANCE
BULL HUNTER
TIGER MAN
GUN GENTLEMEN
THE MUSTANG HERDER
WESTERN TOMMY
SPEEDY
THE WHITE WOLF
TROUBLE IN TIMBERLINE
TIMBAL GULCH TRAIL
THE BELLS OF SAN FILIPO
MARBLEFACE
THE RETURN OF THE RANCHER
RONICKY DOONE'S REWARD
RONICKY DOONE'S TREASURE
RONICKY DOONE

MAX BRAND

SAFETY McTEE

LEISURE BOOKS   NEW YORK CITY

A LEISURE BOOK®

June 1999

Published by special arrangement with Golden West Literary Agency.

Dorchester Publishing Co., Inc.
276 Fifth Avenue
New York, NY 10001

ISBN 0-8439-4528-1

TABLE OF CONTENTS

LITTLE SAMMY GREEN

"Little Sammy Green" first appeared in *Western Story Magazine* (6/30/23), about the same time that the Max Brand serial, "Dan Barry's Daughter," began running in *Argosy* (6/30/23–8/4/23). Sammy Green is anything but a capable gunfighter, but, nonetheless, he must come to terms with his fears by accepting the possibility of death. In the process it is discovered that a most capable gunfighter is far from free of such fears. This short novel appears here for the first time in paperback since its original magazine publication.

Chapter One

"A Summons for Sammy"

"Sammy," said Mr. Green, as supper drew toward a close, "I'll see you in the office after I get through eating."

At this the eyes of Sammy's four big brothers and his mother turned solemnly upon him. Even when he was a rancher, Mr. Green had set apart one room in the ranch house to serve as an office. For he felt that no man could be really dignified or respectable in the eyes of his family unless he had a stated sanctum in which he could retire. And Mr. Green stood solidly upon his dignity on all occasions.

To be sure, there had been but a few uses to which he could turn his office, but he made a point of retiring to it at the end of every day. There he sat at a desk in which he kept his papers—papers that would have been far more at home in a safe. At this desk he smoked a solemn pipe or two and considered the Green affairs. Above all, it was into the office that he invited his children when they were to be punished for crimes of the day.

Mr. Green was not one of those who whip a child as soon as there is an offense. Instead, he waited until the day closed. Then he received from his wife a minutely detailed recital of all the wrongdoings throughout the day. These he added up. If they equaled a whipping, he brought the culprit into the office, stated briefly and clearly the reasons for the punishment, and then laid on the rod, the sparing of which is said to spoil the child.

When a gloomy event forced Mr. Green to give up ranching and retire to the town, where he operated a general merchandise store, the house in which he lived was rather small and crowded by his family of maturing sons; but still he insisted that one corner of the dwelling be kept for his office. There he installed his scarred desk, and to that desk he retired regularly every night after supper and smoked a pipe of reflection; to that desk, also, he called in his sons when he wished to point out their shortcomings, and the tongue of Mr. Green was far more dreadful than his whip. Therefore, it was that the pairs of solemn eyes were fixed upon Sammy. But Sammy only blinked, shrugged his shoulders, and asked for a second piece of pie.

One could hardly imagine a calamity so great that Sammy's mind could be brought away from the contemplation of green-apple pie. In spite of his gastronomic powers, he remained the runt of the family. He had always been the runt. He was the eldest, and, therefore, he had been endowed with his father's own name of Samuel. But how few of Mr. Green's characteristics descended upon the thin shoulders of his son! Who, for instance, could imagine even the nearest and dearest of Mr. Green's old friends calling him by any appellation more familiar than that of Samuel, unshortened by a single syllable.

It was not so, alas, with his offspring. Young Samuel, Jr., had hardly started to school before he was branded Sammy.

When the tidings came home, his father took him into the office and warmed him thoroughly with the rod. Then he sent him back to the school the next day to remove the stigma upon the Green name.

To be called Sam for short was bad enough, but to be degraded by the application of such a diminutive as Sammy was a shock that the worthy Mr. Green could not endure. He told Samuel, Jr., to fight and keep on fighting until the stigma was removed. But Samuel came back the next evening and reported that it was useless to persevere in battle when one was always thrashed. As he had a pair of black eyes and a swollen jaw, his father was forced to take him at his word. That instant, however, he prophesied a shameful life for his son in the future. No man, he said, carrying about such a wretched title as Sammy could ever be looked upon as an equal by self-respecting cowpunchers or men of affairs.

It was with this handicap, therefore, that Sammy entered upon the long adventure of life, and it was not the least of his demerits, in the eyes of Mr. Green, that Sammy failed to realize that the nickname was any handicap at all. For he turned out to be a child of the most irresistible high spirits. His tears would stop almost the instant the rod ceased to fall, and five minutes later he would be blowing at his harmonicon. That mouth organ inspired his dear mother with the conviction that her son had the spark of musical genius in his active bones, but, when three music teachers in succession had given him up as a bad job, it was admitted that the tastes of Sammy in music, as in all other things, were naturally low. He preferred to blow forth on his mouth organ music that was partially made up of remembered strains of dances he had overheard and partly of original phrases of his own, which were almost universally admitted to be very bad, indeed.

So Sammy grew up. He avoided effort on all occasions. Noticeably in his work at school Sammy did just enough to keep from the danger of staying two years in any one grade.

Not that he would have considered failure to be promoted as a disgrace, but because Sammy did not wish to stay in the school any longer than was necessary. Since he had to go through six grades—the goal established by their father as being "good enough for any boy, and all I got myself, and I guess I ain't a fool"—he was determined to finish it as quickly as possible. But since extra effort did not necessarily mean a shortening of the terms, he worked just hard enough to keep from two years in a single grade.

This fairly represented his attitude in all other things. In the school yard Sammy sat in the sunniest corners and blinked at the other boys playing their games. He often used to declare that he got more fun out of watching a game than the other boys got out of playing it. This, in fact, was one of the statements which had caused his father to brand him a born fool. For Mr. Green believed in frankness. He always spoke out his mind in the most forthright fashion, saying frequently that there was no sin in honesty. He could bludgeon any of his children into tears with mere words when he lapsed into his most honest mood; but Sammy remained the exception. He would cant his long, narrow, ugly head upon one side and seem to agree with the statements in a most impersonal, detached fashion.

Once his father had bellowed at him: "Are you listening to your flesh and blood father talk, or are you reading in a book?"

Let it not be considered, however, that Sammy dreamed his way into manhood. By no means. For, though he was quiescent of body, he was as active as a cat with his eyes. Nothing ever missed him. People were always sure that he had understood them, even when he never said a word of comment. And the result was that he was disliked with wonderful unanimity throughout the community. The preacher could not dine at the Green table and pour forth his usual platitudes, which made the head of the household nod and made the lady of the house smile and make her eyes bright, for in the middle of a platitude came a glance from the keen, black eyes of Sammy Green and pricked the bubble of the minister's illusion and made him stammer back to earth. Or, if one of Sammy's brothers started to tell a lie, one of Sammy's steady looks would reduce him to confusion and then to confession. If the rest of the world disliked Sammy, his own brothers hated him.

What could be said of his mother? That good woman did not herself know. Had anyone suggested that she did not love any of her children and that she loved one of them a whit less than any of her others, she would have held up her hands in horror. She could not have analyzed her emotions about Sammy. For good Mrs. Green was so bound around with convention that she had not the slightest idea what she herself felt about anything. She lived by the book, turned up her eyes and her hands at the correct moments, slaved for her husband and her five boys without ever dreaming that it was slavery, and, all in all, lived the life of the million dear blind souls who imitate the actions of rational creatures so exactly as to seem rational themselves.

Perhaps in the entire county there was only one person who suspected the truth about Mrs. Green, and that was Sammy. She herself suspected him. What he could know about her that was shameful she did not know, but sometimes when his steady, gleaming eyes were upon her, she was wretched without knowing why.

To complete the picture of the family, there were four other boys who were already as tall as their father and promised one day to be fully as bulky. And they promised to be as like him in mind as they were already in body.

Supper being ended, the signal for the dispersal of the family was given by Mr. Samuel Green, who pushed his armchair noisily back from the table. One of his devoted sons gave him one crutch; one gave him another. And, tucking the padded heads under the pits of his arms, he swung away toward the office followed by Sammy Green, who was blowing softly on his harmonicon and making so dim a ghost of a tune that no ear but his own heard it.

Instantly the rest of the family formed a conclave for discussion.

"What can the trouble be that Samuel should be so glum about it?" asked the mother.

And Bill Green made answer in his father's own deep bass voice: "I dunno . . . but I think maybe the governor is tired of the way Sammy does things."

"What things?" asked Mrs. Green. "What things, William?"

For her husband had taught her to shorten no names of her children. Dignity, dignity was the thing.

"I dunno what things, except everything," said Bill.

"Everything? Everything?" echoed his mother. "How you talk, child!"

"Ain't I ever going to be called a man?" growled Bill.

"Like enough you are," sighed Mrs. Green. "When children get so growed up that they can't help their mother with the supper dishes, I guess it's time enough to call them men."

There was no irony in her meaning. She spoke, as always, simply and from the heart. And her sons accepted her words in that sense. But, afterward, the four boys found occasion to walk stealthily past the door of the office to hear what was passing. That was not a hard matter, for Mr. Samuel Green always spoke in a single tone which was close to the top of his lung power.

Chapter Two

"Banished"

The moment that they were alone in the office, Mr. Green said: "I got something to say to you, Sammy, that's been growing in my head for the saying for about twenty-two years."

Since Sammy was exactly twenty-two, it was not hard to guess the subject on which the mind of his father had been turning for so long a period. But now Mr. Green allowed suspense to accumulate, while he filled his deep pipe, packing in every shred of the tobacco carefully. After he had lighted the pipe, he frowned at Sammy through the cloud of smoke, like a grim-faced idol behind a mist of incense.

"When that skunk, Harry Link, got the drop on me and filled me full of lead," he said, "what did you do?"

He was referring to the disaster which had caused him to leave off ranching in the neighboring county. His repute as a cow raiser, to be sure, had always been less formidable than his fame as a gunfighter, and his pride in his skill with weapons had always been far greater than his pride in his Herefords. So it happened that an ambitious young man, who wished to establish himself as a warrior of might, could think of no better way of testing his metal and proving his gallantry in the eyes of the community than by encountering Green in single combat. This was Harry Link, who met Green on a day and exchanged with him certain winged words. They wound up their argument by reaching for guns. Then it was that the rancher, for the first time in his life, was fairly beaten to the draw. He always referred to the battle as the scene of Harry Link's treachery, but all the rest of the community knew that it had been a fair fight, and the wounds were Samuel Green's—the glory was the glory of Harry Link. He became the foremost fighting man in the county at a single stroke, and Mr. Green brooded over his loss of position until he decided to move into a new domain. So he had sold the ranch and departed. But he had done this only after his four big sons had assailed Harry Link, had been routed by him with various and sundry wounds, and had been driven back to their home.

They arrived in the town where Mr. Green set up his general merchandise store and prospered on the score of his fame as a warrior until another youth of swelling ambitions, named Louis Mariscal, appeared on the scene. To him Mr. Green now referred.

"And when Louis Mariscal took me by surprise and broke my leg with a bullet, what did you do?"

It was so apparent that he did not expect an answer, that Sammy did not attempt to give one. He simply blew meditatively into his harmonicon and brought forth a thin and whistling melody.

"Stop that infernal noise!" said Mr. Green.

Sammy wrapped the mouth organ in a silk handkerchief, placed the instrument in his pocket, wiped his lips with his sleeve, and prepared to do nothing but listen.

"I suppose I didn't do nothing," he admitted, since words were now demanded.

"You suppose? You know right well that you didn't do nothing. You let your brothers go out and try to get revenge on the hound, and you stayed warm at home!"

"I s'pose I did."

"Glory in it, don't you?"

"Nope."

"I say you do. Tickles you to show that you don't care none for your own father!"

Sammy was silent and watched his father's face curiously, after his habit. He might have been thinking of almost anything. But his father construed the thoughts in the most disagreeable possible fashion.

"You thought what the rest of the blockheads thought, that Mariscal beat me fair and square, eh?"

"I ain't said that."

"You ain't said it. You never say nothing. You keep your thinking inside of your head and let it go at that. But *I* know you . . . I read you like a book. You ain't too deep for your father to foller you and your ways!"

He beat out these words with a huge fist upon the top of his desk, and his bullet-scarred face twitched with fury. As a matter of fact, he had struck upon the truth. Louis Mariscal, just as Harry Link had done, had found fame for himself in a single day by beating Samuel Green. Since that time the glory of Mariscal and the glory of Link had grown and grown until their fields of reputation were beginning to overlap. People said that they would have to settle the question of supremacy by encountering each other one of these days, but apparently they still respected each other's prowess too much to have the engagement. They contented themselves with talking scornfully of one another. In the meantime, as the men who had conquered him showed themselves more and more formidable by their later actions, the sting of defeat was somewhat lessened in the mind of Samuel Green, but he remained with a sad reminder of his last battle in the shape of the broken leg, the bone of which had failed to heal, and he had been condemned to crutches for the rest of his life. He thought of all these things, as he stared bitterly at Sammy. His four other boys had all gone out and collected scars in attempting to avenge him. Only this rascal sluggard had remained at home in the warmest nook of the kitchen.

He was the oldest son, but he was the only one who deigned to wipe the dishes for his old mother. That, in the mind of the father, fixed the standing of Sammy once and for all time.

"I been holding back for along time," went on Mr. Green. "I been hoping against hope that you'd up and mend your ways one of these days. But I ain't seen no change in sight, and it's about time for me to act. Today I aim to say what I got inside of my head!"

"Go ahead," said Sammy. "But ain't you got the makings of a cigarette?"

There was a roar of rage from Mr. Green, but Sammy did not wince. Instead, he yawned in the face of the irate old hero and prepared himself sleepily to listen. Suddenly the arm of Mr. Green shot out. He transfixed Sammy, so to speak, with the accusing point of his forefinger.

"What you thinking of right this here minute?" he demanded hoarsely.

"Of green-apple pie," admitted Sammy.

"Barking dogs!" exclaimed Mr. Green, as he turned away with his gesture, as though appealing to the world.

"Mother has the world beat for pie," declared Sammy.

"Pie!" thundered Mr. Green.

"Don't you think so?" said Sammy.

"I've come to talk about you, not about a fool thing like pie!"

"I'm listening with all my might," nodded Sammy, and stared at a cobweb in a far corner that had escaped the vigilant hand of Mrs. Green. Certainly the years were bowing her spirit.

"When we was on the ranch," said Mr. Green, "how many cows did you rope?"

"I dunno," said Sammy. "You know that I never was no good with figures."

"Fire and brimstone!" bellowed the tormented father. "Ain't you going to admit that you never learned to use a rope at all during the years that you was out there?"

Here Sammy inclined his head to the side and frowned in deep thought. Even when he smiled, his face was homely enough, but, when he frowned, he was so ugly that he seemed almost formidable, even in the eyes of his father.

"Didn't never seem to have no talent for the using of a rope," admitted Sammy at last.

"Let the roping go. How many hosses did you break all the time that you was living out on the range?"

"I disremember," said Sammy mildly.

"You do? Well, son, *I* remember. And what I remember is that the sum total of all the hosses that you ever broke was just exactly *none!*"

"You don't say!" exclaimed Sammy sympathetically.

"Well, ain't I right?"

"Near as I can remember, I guess that you are."

"You're still guessing about it! I'm all through guessing about you. But I'm going to make you admit everything. When we come into town and started in the store, what was your first job in it?"

"Don't exactly recollect."

"You don't? You started in selling the agricultural implements," said the father.

"That's right. You got a great head for remembering, Dad."

"D'you remember how much you sold in three months?"

"The long names of some of the parts of them machines was a little too much for me," said Sammy blandly.

17

"You sold one rake," said Mr. Green. He writhed in his seat, furious at the memory. "One two-hoss rake was the sum total of all the selling that you done in that department of the store."

"Well, well," said Sammy. "I disremembered of selling anything, but I guess that you're right."

The father clenched his teeth so tightly that the stem of his pipe was shattered. He removed the pieces, one by one. It was a very old pipe. He had smoked it for five years, and the stem was covered with the prints of his teeth. Now he laid aside the parts of the ruined stem in silence. His fury was beginning to be a sacred thing, too great for any words to contain it.

"Where did you go from the implement department?" asked the father, speaking in a choked fashion.

"Lemme see . . . ," drawled Sammy.

"You started selling dry goods. You got all the sizes mixed. You forgot all the prices. Didn't you try to sell a pair of overalls for forty dollars, and didn't Simpson, what you tried to sell 'em to, come raving to me, and call me a crook and a thief?"

"I got a hazy sort of recollection of something like that," said Sammy. "Seems to me that I got the size number mixed up with the price."

"Bah!" groaned the poor father. "Sammy, have you got any brains at all?"

"I dunno," said Sammy. "I never had no call to use them."

At this retort Mr. Green lifted himself from his chair by his arms alone, glared at his son, and then lowered himself again.

"You're fired!" he shouted.

Sammy grinned.

"You can't do it," he said. "You never hired me."

"Are you mocking me?" thundered Samuel Green. "I

say, I disown you from this minute! Never show your face inside of the walls of my house again."

"I got the makings, after all," said Sammy smoothly. "Darned, if I didn't plumb overlook them."

With that he produced from a vest pocket a sack of tobacco and a few crumpled brown papers, one of which he smoothed out to receive the tobacco.

"I dunno," said his father slowly, "I dunno whether I'd ought to hate you or pity you, Sammy."

"Well," said Sammy, "I dunno, but what I could say the same thing for you ... but I won't. I found out about you some time back!"

The rage of Samuel Green made it impossible for him to speak for a few minutes. When his voice came, Sammy was at the door. Here he turned and made his father entirely speechless by a few parting words.

"If you get in bad trouble," he said, "always just send for me, and I'll come back and fix you all up."

Then he went out to the kitchen and said good bye to his mother. She threw her arms around his neck and wept on his shoulder until Mr. Green came swinging out on his crutches and bade her loose her son from her arms and shut him out of her house and heart forever.

She obeyed. How could she have broken a twenty-three-year old habit of obedience?

"But, oh, Sammy," she moaned, "what have you been doing to your father?"

"Listening to him," said Sammy thoughtfully. "That's about the worst thing anybody could do for the governor."

Chapter Three

"The Rise of a Reputation"

It took Sammy five minutes to collect his belongings into a
small bag, say good bye to his brothers, and leave the place.
No one seemed to regret his leaving, save an old short-haired
fox terrier that waddled after him to the corner of the first
quarter-section fence on the road away from town. There,
panting and shaking his fat sides from the effort, he licked
his hand, whined after him, and turned slowly back to the
Green house. Sammy watched the dog go out of sight around
the next bend of the road, and then he walked on until he
came to Middleburg, eight miles off and on the railroad. He
rode the freight out of Middleburg at midnight and was
thrown off by a profane brakeman the next morning, as the
train climbed into the mountains.

Luckily he was only five miles from another town when
he hit the cinders beside the freight. He made that haven by

noon, bought himself a meal with his last fifty cents, and went to the employment agency.

He found a dozen men there before him. Half of them were cowpunchers, and half of them were lumbermen—big men such as befitted a big country, rough men such as befitted a rough country. They gave Sammy a single volley of glances, and then his nearest neighbor summed him up with a question: "What job you aiming at, son . . . roustabout?"

Some men would have fought on less provocation than that, but Sammy had learned in his schooldays that the fists of other people are hard and land with painful effect. So he did not fight. He merely grinned and rolled a cigarette, drawing his chair back into the corner, so that he could be less easily observed. In this fashion, with the shadow falling across him, he could study the others at his leisure, and the more he saw of them the more he was certain that he had come into a strange land. For they were all blunt and briefspoken men. Their chests swelled out with a noble indication of lung power, and their hands were as big as the hands of sailors.

In half an hour an employer came in. By the man who ran the employment agency he was hailed as Ira Burnside. He seemed in no haste to announce his purpose until he had first looked over all the men in the room. He seemed to know most of the cowpunchers. He called three or four by name, and, after he had chatted with them, he asked the crowd in general if any of them wished to come up to his ranch. There was a silence in response, and at last one fellow spoke up for the rest.

"We like your pay and your job fine, Burnside," he said, "but we ain't got any liking for the fixings that go along with that there job you got to offer!"

There was a general laugh at this, and Burnside joined in the mirth in a rather sour-faced fashion.

"What sort of fixings does he mean?" asked Sammy of

his nearest neighbor who had put him so thoroughly in his place. The latter looked down at him with an eloquent contempt.

"That place ain't for you, son," he said. "Don't go busting your heart trying to find out about it. Just let things ride easy. By the way, I think that old Gus wants a dishwasher over to the hotel."

These were gratuitous insults, but the big 'puncher added to them at once. "Besides," he said, "even if your wanted that there job, Burnside wouldn't take you. He's got a real eye for men."

Sammy rose and yawned. "Are you a gambling man?" he asked.

"I've played a few games in my time. Is that your line?"

"What would you bet, now, that Burnside don't hire me?"

"Five dollars," said the other.

"I'll take that," said Sammy.

"Let's see your money."

"I guess this is worth five dollars," said Sammy, and he produced a long and shimmering Colt revolver from a holster.

"Ah!" murmured the other. Only that, but there was in his voice all the respect that instantly springs into the bosom of a man who knows guns when he sees a well-cleaned and well-oiled weapon in the hands of another.

"I shall know a man by the books he owns," said one.

"I shall know a man by the sheen of the bore of his rifle," said another.

"That's worth five dollars right enough. By the way, my name is Owen."

"I'm glad to know your name," said Sammy, and, looking the other in the eye, he refrained from either giving his own name or holding forth his hand.

It might have been called the affront direct, but Owen was not quite ready to resent it. His brain was whirling, as if he had caught a rabbit and seen it turn on him with the teeth of a bloodthirsty ferret.

"And I'll be wondering," said Sammy, "what sort of a bet you'll make that I don't stay on his ranch with him?"

But Owen had enough of this mysterious and slender man. He was not of the type of the others who were punching cows in that neighborhood and, because he was different, Owen was willing to give him plenty of distance. So Sammy went up to the rancher.

"Mister Burnside," he said, "if you're plumb anxious to have a cowman, gimme a try."

Burnside looked down into Sammy's face. "What can you do?" he asked.

"I can take a hand," said Sammy wisely.

"Can you rope?"

"Nothing to speak about."

"Are you wise to the range? Good at riding range?" asked Burnside.

"I can ride," said Sammy with such artlessness that every man in the room laughed, with one exception, which was Owen.

"You can ride? Breaking hosses your line?"

"I dunno that I've ever broke any," said Sammy.

"I dunno but you'd remember if you ever had done it," mocked Burnside. "Why should I hire you?"

"Because nobody else will go," said Sammy.

It was something of a facer for the other.

"I suppose you're willing?" he suggested.

"I'm ready to learn," said Sammy.

"But I'm running a ranch, not a school."

"That," said Sammy, "is not my fault."

For the first time Burnside regarded him steadily. "You can come along," he said finally. "I've always been willing to play long shots."

This was not particularly flattering, but Sammy Green was looking for shelter and board, not flattery, so that afternoon he drove out over the hills with Burnside in the latter's buckboard. And there were not six words spoken during the journey. For the rancher was very busy with his thoughts, and Sammy Green was very busy with his mouth organ until Burnside requested him in the name of the Deity and as a grace to his fellow men to abandon his music.

So Sammy complied and sat hunched over on the seat, a shapeless figure like a loosely filled sack, his head bobbing on his scrawny neck, as the wagon jolted over the irregularities of the road. They did not reach the ranch until dusk, when they topped a rise and looked down into a broad valley forested in a scattering fashion with big trees, watered with half a dozen creeks that streaked their crooked courses across the meadows, and containing on the side of the hill the house of the rancher. When he saw the estate, Sammy could understand the quality of the two horses that had drawn them out from the town. They were close to Thoroughbreds, with the carriage of eagles and the gait of flowing water, but one who owned a sweep of country as rich as this and as wide could afford to be particular with his stable.

The horses, swinging to the top of the pitch, had paused an instant without word from the driver, as though they also wished to linger an instant in order to enjoy the view. And, as they started down the slope again, Sammy was aware of a ghostly figure swinging up toward him from the gloom of the valley. At the same instant—of course, it was only the most foolish coincidence—the wind bore to his nostrils a breath of pure fragrance of the pines that made his heart leap and his eyes shine. He knew at once it was a girl—and a lovely one. He could not be wrong. His feeling was as sure a sign as though he had seen her before and was remembering her now.

Then she grew out at them. The horse hardly seemed to be touching the ground, as he swung up toward them, but that was because, as Sammy presently saw, the animal was a gray, with dark points—a glorious horse that floated over the road toward them. And then came the girl. It wasn't white that she wore, but a rich cream-colored habit, not deep enough for tan. It was like the color of her skin, without the glow of the cheeks to light it, or the shining of the eyes. For it actually seemed to the strange mind of Sammy Green, as he watched her coming on, that she was illumined from within.

He registered that emotion, and then he looked religiously away from her, above her to the sky where the stars were beginning to walk out, here singly, here in lively clusters.

"This is a new hand, Sammy Green, Kathleen," said the rancher.

And Sammy decided that Kathleen was the best name in the world, and that it had been cunningly invented and then kept in waiting until she should come, who filled all of its connotations, as the rightful hand plumps out the glove.

"He's a hoss buster that ain't never remembered breaking a hoss, and a 'puncher that ain't ever remembered roping a cow," said the rancher, as he laughed at his jest.

"For all of that," said the girl gravely, "brave men are what you want, Dad. I'm glad to know you, Sammy Green."

Twice that night Sammy wakened and found his own voice saying: "I'm glad to know you, Sammy Green." He found himself saying it with the greatest emotion and conviction, as though it were a great discovery. And each time he sighed himself to sleep.

When he awakened in the morning, he found that there was a good deal to be observed. In the first place, his fellow cowpunchers were the roughest lot he had ever seen. There was not one of them who did not show the scars of battle in his face, and in his eyes the gleam of the battle light that is unmistakable. Sammy regarded them in his own quiet and insistent way until it seemed that he was trying to recognize in each of them some old acquaintance.

As for their manner of greeting him, it was most amusing. They apparently could not understand how anyone, saving a formidable fighter, could have been brought out to the ranch, and, therefore, they took it for granted that Sammy Green was a warrior of fame. The rancher fostered the joke. He dropped hints here and there, which in the words were nothing, but which in the intonation inferred that Sammy Green had done strange things in his time. And the tall cowpunchers listened and nodded to one another and believed.

For, just as Owen had noticed the day before in the employment agency, this man was different. His voice, his words, his manner were different. And whereas his silence might have been taken for meekness by some, by others it might well be interpreted as the quiet of the most terrible of killers, the man who strikes without warning.

So it was that the cowpunchers of the Burnside ranch were prepared to accept the stranger. It mattered not that he was so unhandy with a rope that he could hardly catch his own mount in the morning. It mattered not that he seemed almost as though he were afraid of his horse. For who does not know that often those who are the most heroic with their fellow men are deadly afraid of the spider that crawls over their boots, or the little dog that yelps behind the calf of their leg? The more peculiarities Sammy Green showed, the more closely regarded he was.

They waited for two days before they approached the silence of Sammy. Then it was on a matter concerning a revolver. But Sammy put them off. As a matter of fact, he knew nothing about a revolver except that he could clean one. His father had employed him almost from infancy in that work, so that he could take down a Colt with his eyes blinded and assemble it again with marvelous deftness. But as for using the little mechanism of destruction, he had very little idea of it.

However, the cowpunchers reported to one another that when Sammy was riding by himself, his revolver was constantly heard at work. And so it was, for Sammy was working desperately to gain in a few days the practice which might prove to be so necessary to him before he was off the ranch. All of the men were furnished with as much ammunition as they wished by the rancher. It fitted perfectly with Burnside's plans that they should practice as much as they chose, and they could help themselves to cartridges by the handful. They could ride out every morning with a double belt of bullets and come home with it empty in the evening, if they chose. That was exactly what Sammy was doing, and his results were a tired wrist and very few targets hit. But he kept right on blazing away. He felt sure that, if the thousandth chance ever came when he was cornered and *must* resort to a gun play, he would have no time to steady himself for a careful shot. Therefore, he made all of his shots swift and casual. He rode with his gun in the holster until his eye caught on a white spot on a stone, or a squirrel standing up like a little peg near his hole. Then he snatched out the gun and fired—all in one motion and as fast as his hand could jump. But he missed, missed, missed!

It was noticed that he plowed up a good deal of wood at a distance from the knot in the trees which must have been his targets, but the other men explained this readily enough by deciding that he was one of those devilishly clever gunfighters who can use their skill to pick off a man by placing their bullets in spots where the results will not be mortal. He was a man who considered his target as the head of the man, and, with that as a center, he fired at imaginary arms and legs.

But Sammy kept on practicing and missing for a week. And every evening, when he came in, he sat on his bunk with a little board across his knees and oil and rags and all that he needed on the board. Then he began to take down the gun, and his eyes never followed what his deft fingers were doing. The other cowpunchers watched him, enchanted. They had seen other men do strange things with bullets, but this was a new game with a gun, and it bespoke a familiarity with the weapon that was worth worship and fear, indeed!

Not one of them but could blow out the heart of a target with snap shots; but this was all new, this dexterous work in which it seemed that each finger possessed separate intelligence. So they smoked their cigarettes in a silent awe and said nothing to Sammy Green and thought the more. Rumor of their state of mind came to the rancher, and he called Sammy to him.

"Sammy Green," he said, "what the devil is all this talk I hear from the bunkhouse about you being a man-killer?"

"I never called myself a man-killer," said Sammy.

"Never called yourself that . . . just named some of the men that you killed?" suggested Burnside.

And his daughter, who was reading in a corner of the library, looked up and over the edge of her book, and Sammy saw that her eyes were great and round. It almost stopped his heart, that glance at her. But alas, if she knew the truth about him, would she look at him twice? If she knew that he was only a stupid blunderer. . . .

"I disremember," said Sammy, "ever telling them the name of any man I killed."

At this Burnside started. "By the Lord, Green," he said, "are you something besides a joke?"

It was too much by far in the presence of Kathleen.

"I don't quite foller you," said Sammy slowly. "Did you say something or other about a joke?"

Burnside broke into hearty laughter. "Why, you little. . . ."

"I'm listening patient, trying to make out what you might've said," said Sammy, with the same careful slowness. "I don't want to make no useless trouble."

"Why, what the devil do you . . . ," began Burnside, but, here, there was a shrill cry from Kathleen, and then her slender body flashed between her father and the young cowpuncher.

"Don't answer him!" she cried. "Don't anger him, Dad . . . dear Dad! Don't you see what he is? He's a killer! He's a killer! Oh, Dad, he's planning to murder you this instant!'' And, throwing her arms around the neck of her father, she burst into tears upon his shoulder.

"Cows and little fishes," muttered Burnside, glowering at Sammy. But here he paused. His anger faded into a sort of dark dismay. "Green," he said, "you *are* a gunfighter!"

"I never in my life made no such statement."

"I didn't say you were a blowhard. I said you were a handy man with a gun. Well, you're welcome here. I need all I can get of 'em. But, now, tell this silly girl that there ain't nothing in what she's been fearing for me."

"Lady," said Sammy Green, "I never used a gun on a gent in my life."

It was the truth. It could not have been a more solemn truth had he searched his mind for one. But the rancher broke into laughter again, laughter of a different quality.

"You don't have to stretch it as much as all that," he assured Sammy. "There ain't no need of lying, Sammy."

Chapter Four

"The Offer"

Such was the manner in which Sammy Green's repute as a gunman arose. And it was not tested at once. To be sure, the others tried in every known way to lure him into an exhibition of his skill, but he always told them mildly that he did not use a revolver a great deal. This manifest lie, when they could hear his gun popping on the range every day, had to be swallowed with a smile, unless they wished to challenge his veracity. And no one was prepared to do that. Their attitude toward Sammy was that of the school yard boys to a newcomer who seems formidable, but who has not yet been tried with the vital test of hard knuckles. This case was the same, except that, here, the question was one of guns and bullets, and, therefore, the hesitation was much longer. Eventually, however, Sammy would have received his testing had it not been for the intervention of a great event.

This was no other than the descent of Maurie Washburn

from the upper mountains. It was expected, this coming of the famous outlaw and cattle rustler. But, nevertheless, it spread dismay throughout the range. He did not come with his usual small group. Instead, he swept down with thrice his ordinary numbers, scooped in a vast herd of cattle, shot and badly wounded three of Burnside's valiant cowpunchers who strove to stem the invasion, and headed the mass of cattle south.

Among the ravines the herd was split into small sections and headed for the markets into which Washburn fed his stolen beef. And behind him he left Burnside on the verge of prostration, so furious was his rage. He stormed at the rear of the outlaw's little army, was thrown back with a bullet furrow in his right cheek and the wounding of two more of his men, one so badly that he nearly bled to death before he was carried to the ranch house.

The result of the whole fracas was that Burnside had five of his best men laid up with wounds, the services of three others needed to care for the injured men, and no one to strike at the rear of the retreating thief—that is, with any chance of success. And by the time his willing neighbors had rallied to his rescue, the tough cattle from his range had been swept far away through the mountain passes.

It was simply another victory for Maurie Washburn over the ranchers, and he had scored so many of them before that he was more or less taken for granted. The only reason that Burnside was somewhat more pitied than others was that he had been the most frequent victim of the outlaw. His range lay nearest to those fastnesses where Washburn assembled his men and prepared to dip like a hawk on his prey, and, therefore, Burnside had been more annoyed than others. It had become more than an annoyance. He was losing his very substance. He calculated, after this last raid, that he had lost all of his profits, beyond mere living, for the past five years, and that the final raid had eaten well into his capital. Therefore, he was ready to fight to the last, and he strove to gather his neighbors together for the same purpose. But it was hard to rally them. They had suffered less than he, and the expense of maintaining a whole body of high-priced fighters on the trail was more than they cared to undertake.

He found himself greeted with condolences, but with no promises of cash, and, therefore, he turned with a louder wail to the law. But the law was already doing its very best. The worthy sheriff of that county was a man in a thousand, ready to fight a mountain full of bandits and ready to die in the performance of his duty, but, when he attacked Washburn, his talk was hard. For Maurie Washburn was not supported by his gang alone. He had purchased friends throughout the mountains with gifts of a few cattle here and a little money there, until he could hardly ride a league without stumbling upon a supporter. And these men were always ready to throw dust in the eyes of the men of the law when the latter came upon the trail of Washburn. According to the size of his train was the difficulty of apprehending him. And though the sheriff campaigned valiantly, he campaigned in vain. In fact, there was a saying in the mountains that Maurie Washburn would never be taken until one man turned up who would be willing to try the task, but where a crowd came, it was simple for Maurie to slip away from them faster than they could possibly approach.

Who the one man could be who would be capable of undertaking such a feat no one could venture to suggest. For instance, it would have been suicide for the kind old sheriff to attack Maurie hand to hand. For though he had the heart of a lion, his eyes were failing him, and the hands that had once been so strong and so sure were tremulous with years. He was still a great leader, but he was no longer a great warrior. The best he could do was to bring swift-flying posses upon the trail, but the posses broke their teeth in vain against the mountain traps into which Maurie Washburn disappeared. He still went free, and the hero who was to capture the desperado, or else kill him in single combat, was as far in the future as ever before.

Such were the remarks which were heard at the long table in the dining room of the ranch house, where the unwounded members of the Burnside outfit gathered for the noon meal. All hopes of trailing Washburn down were now gone, so far as the last outrage was concerned.

"But when the right man comes along," said Lefty, who was the oldest and the best cowpuncher on the place, "when the right man comes along, this here Washburn ain't going to go down no harder than a hundred others just like him. He ain't going to be no grizzly bear that takes a ton of lead for killing him. Maybe some kid that nobody ain't heard of yet will up and take the job on his hands."

And, as he said this, he turned his glance down the table. There was a sudden silence. And Sammy Green, looking mildly up and over the edge of his thick coffee cup, found that all glances were focused upon him.

A terrible moment. He could have endured the eyes of the men, but, when the battery was joined by the steady and serious eyes of Kathleen Burnside, it was another matter entirely. It seemed to Sammy Green that her glance entered his soul through his eyes and there weighed it, waiting to learn whether or not it was lacking in weight.

He had not fully realized how completely the others were bluffed. For them he was content to let the bluff stand, but for Kathleen. . . . No doubt she was afraid of him, rather than attracted to him, but to be feared was a delightful sensation to Sammy Green. It made his brain spin around with happiness.

And he said in his sad heart: *Of course, I'm just what Dad always used to say . . . I'm a coward. I ain't no good. It ain't no use for me to pretend even to myself. I just ain't got any courage. Sooner or later they'll all be sure to find it out, but I sure wish that time would never come to Kathleen. I sure wish that.*

When the dinner was over, he strolled slowly outside and walked up and down under a big tree that stood at the rear of the ranch house. Some white leghorns came up and scratched in the dust, unfearful of his boots, so soft and regular was his step. And, as he walked with his thoughts, he heard the voice of Burnside talking among the cowpunchers and saying: "It ain't a question of just getting revenge on him. It's a question of whether I go broke or not. That's what it is! If he stays around in this neck of the woods and in this part of the country, then I'm through. Ira Burnside goes bust, if Maurie Washburn keeps on rustling cattle. I can't keep right on raising cattle for charity!"

"It's a rotten shame," muttered one of the boys.

"Ain't it?" said another. "I guess you'd just about give twenty thousand dollars to get rid of Washburn, eh, chief?"

Burnside paused. "Twenty thousand dollars . . . for Washburn?" he cried, in a sort of ecstasy of impatience. "I'll tell you what, boys, just what I'd do. I'll give you the straight of it, hey, Kathleen."

Kathleen appeared at the door of the dining room that opened out upon the verandah. Her face was dark behind the screen.

"You come right on out here, honey. I got something to say that I want to hear you talk about, too."

She stepped out upon the porch and came slowly toward him, and, as she stood in the steep shadow of the porch, it seemed to Sammy Green again that she was lighted from within by a sacred and lovely light.

"Boys," said the rancher, now that his daughter was nearby, "I want you to know that to the gent that kills or captures Washburn . . . and I guess that there ain't no chance of him being taken alive . . . I'll give one half of everything that I got here. I'll give him one half of the profits of everything that I make each year. And I'll try to guarantee him a half interest in the place after I die, because I'll try to marry him to Kathleen."

"Dad!" cried Kathleen.

"Save your blushing for later on," said her father. "Answer up to me straight and quick . . . wouldn't you marry the gent that was man enough to kill Maurie Washburn?"

And then it seemed to Sammy Green that she shook back her shoulders and drew herself away from, and above, her weaker self.

"A man . . . a man who was big and brave-hearted enough to capture that . . . that demon!" cried Kathleen. "How could a girl keep from marrying him?"

"You see?" echoed the rancher. "You see what I mean, now? There ain't any bluff in this. I mean every word of it. I'd give Kathleen, and you hear her, up there, saying that she'd be plumb willing to be given to the lucky gent. Well, boys, that's all the reward that I offer. I've been working for five years for Washburn . . . for that skunk! I been his slave! And, sooner'n keep it up, I'll sell out and move!"

It was a grim statement. It was as impossible for the cowpunchers to imagine that section of the country without the Burnside fortune and the Burnside name as it would be to conceive the West with the Rockies plucked out by the roots.

And all afternoon, as he rode the line of fence to which he had been assigned for that day—since even Sammy could drive in staples and tighten loose strands of the wire—he kept turning the thing over in his mind, he kept calling up the picture of the young hero who would destroy the outlaw. That night, when he came in, he went straight to Burnside.

"What you said this noon . . . ," he began.

"Are you thinking of going out and trying your luck on Washburn?" asked the rancher kindly.

And his kindness made Sammy Green look up in amazement. Did he not know himself? Did he not know that he himself was slender and bowed of shoulders and long and ugly of face? Did he not know himself for a caricature? He flushed a little.

"You meant what you said about giving Kathleen to the

gent that would get rid of Maurie Washburn?'' he asked faintly.

"I sure did, son! You go out and do your best. I ain't going to stop your wages while you're on that there trail!''

Chapter Five

"Sammy Rides South"

How blind, how blind he was, thought Sammy Green, as he went away. And how could a man even dream of promising his daughter to such a fellow as himself, in case blind luck or mere skill of hand should favor him?

He began to cast about in his mind for the proper man. It would be a crime above all others he could imagine, if the wrong man should win Kathleen. He drew a picture of the hero. Kathleen was small, to be sure. Had she been larger, it would hardly have been possible to imagine so much grace and such a jewel finish as she possessed. But the man to marry her must be large. Sammy Green had always worshipped the idea of a big man. When he was a child he had always dreamed of growing into great thews and bones. He had always pictured his mature self as a veritable giant.

And, even now, whenever he saw himself in the mirror, there was a wrench of pain at the strings of his heart. The man must be tall and powerful, then, who was to marry Kathleen. And in the second place, he must be handsome, so that they would make a seemly couple. Yes, he must be handsome, too—probably with blond hair, a tawny mane of it, and keen blue eyes to contrast with the dark hair and the deep brown eyes of Kathleen.

And, as he drew the picture, suddenly the very man who filled the requirements of the sketch jumped into his thoughts. He knew the man, the man above all others who must win Kathleen. That night, when the other men were asleep in the bunkhouse, he rose and went down to the corrals. There he found his horse and saddled the animal and rode straight south until the morning. When the morning came, he put up at a ranch house, fed the horse, ate breakfast, slept a short sleep, and drove south again.

At the Burnside place they would say that he had gone on the trail of the outlaw. Let them say what they pleased. He would have the results accomplished before he showed himself again at the ranch, or, he would start the stone in motion, and, while it was rolling, he would go back to the ranch and wait for the accomplishment of the task. A sad glory to see the woman he loved married to another, and yet how much better to know that her husband was a true hero, and not a mere brute.

So, on the third day, he rode his weary horse up to a small shack in the evening and tapped at the door. In answer to the knock, the door was thrown open, and there appeared a young giant with a tawny head of hair and keen blue eyes and shoulders that jammed the doorway full. At the sight of Sammy Green, however, he exclaimed and whipped out a gun, but Sammy raised his hands instantly above the level of his shoulders.

"I ain't come here for trouble, Louis Mariscal," he said. "I've come here as your friend. I've come here to tell you the best news that ever you heard. Will you lemme come in and talk to you?"

And the man who had made his reputation at the expense of terrible Samuel Green, hastily shoved his gun back into the holster, as though ashamed. Then he stepped back from the door and waved his guest inside.

"You just gave me a sort of start when I first seen you," he confessed shamefacedly. "You see, your brothers have come gunning for me so often that, when I see the face of a Green, I just sort of nacherally reached for the Colt. Sit down and rest your feet, Sammy."

Sammy accepted the invitation, and, as he did so, he looked around the shack. It was all he could have wished. The place was small, as befitted the house of a man who was only making his beginning as a rancher, running a small string of cows on the range; but everything was kept as scrupulously neat as though a woman, and a good woman, were in charge of the arrangements. Even the top of the stove was scoured; the pans that hung on the wall were bright; the floor was newly swept; the rag rug had been beaten clean not more than a day before; the blankets on the bunk were faded by washings and not by dirt; and, above all, in the estimation of Sammy, there was a little shelf filled with books. And there were more books on the table, one of them face downward.

"Studying, Louis?" he asked.

"A man has to learn a lot to run a ranch . . . even a mighty small one like I got," said Louis. "I been beating my way through some books on the handling of cows. Some of it is hard going. But, here and there, I pick up a trail where I can sort of read the sign pretty well. It helps. It ain't helping me so much this year as it will five years from now. And how's your folks, Sammy?"

"Me and my folks," said Sammy slowly, "ain't wasting much time on each other. I been run out."

"I heard tell about some sort of trouble," said Louis stiffly.

And there was no more. Another man, Sammy felt, would

39

have taken the opportunity to tell Sammy that his people were a bad lot and that he was glad Sammy had broken away from them. But this was not the way of Louis Mariscal. He waited for Sammy to talk more on that lead, or else to pick up another.

"Maybe you're hungry," he suggested.

"I am," said Sammy.

There was only a shade of hesitation in the face of Louis Mariscal, and Sammy knew what he meant. The big man was afraid that Sammy had come to do by treachery what the rest of the Green family had been unable to do by strength or by skill. Yet, after the instant of pause, he resolutely turned his back on his guest and went about the preparation of a meal. It was quickly got together, and, when the preparations ended, the big man placed the food in tin dishes before Sammy—cold pone and rashers of bacon and steaming coffee and potatoes. Sammy ate until the provisions had disappeared. Then he cleaned his own plate and cup, lighted a cigarette, and tilted his chair back against the wall. In the last pause a coyote had come down out of the hills and was wailing from a nearby arroyo that spirit-thin cry that always seems to come from a great distance.

"Well," said Sammy, "what I come down to talk to you about is your wife."

"I dunno that I foller what you're saying," murmured the startled Mariscal.

"Not yet. You'll understand pretty soon. Figuring on marrying one of these days, ain't you?"

"I s'pose that we all do."

"What would you say to the prettiest girl that ever drew a breath and the finest and the straightest, with a whole big ranch coming her way when her father cashes in?"

"Are you joking, Sammy?"

"Lemme talk!"

And talk he did, until he had told the whole story from

beginning to end. And while he talked, making every point and pouring all of his heart into the story, Louis Mariscal looked him steadily in the eye and puffed at a pipe that cast up before him a thin screen of smoke. Now and then, the pipe tilted a little at some thrilling phrase of description of Kathleen.

When the story was ended, Louis remained quietly in his chair for a time and then rose and walked to the door.

"If I went, I'd have a pretty good chance of getting salted away with lead," he said.

"You sure would."

"And some folks might think that was the main thing that brought you down here . . . just a chance to see me finished up, Sammy."

"Some folks might think that way, but you wouldn't."

"And if I went, it'd mean that I'd be playing for big stakes, and, if I come back here, this layout of mine could look pretty small."

"It would," said Sammy.

"I dunno," murmured Louis.

While he wavered, Sammy played the trump card that he had been keeping up his sleeve for the crisis. He drew out his wallet and, from the wallet, extracted a photograph.

"Louis," he said, "here is her picture," and he laid it in the hand of the big man.

It was late dusk, and the dull light so dimmed the picture that nothing was really distinct in it saving the light of the smile and the light of the eyes. Louis Mariscal drew it close and then held it again at arm's length, all without a word.

"I'll keep that picture," he muttered at length.

"You won't," said Sammy. "That stays with me."

Mariscal gave it thoughtfully back to him.

"Sammy," he said gently at length, "you love her?"

"Too much to see her married to some skunk that can't handle a gun and ain't got a heart."

41

"Suppose you were to get him yourself, Sammy?"

"Me kill Washburn? I got to laugh, partner. Besides, even if I did, what kind of a husband would a shrimp like me make for her?"

Chapter Six

"Friendly Enemies"

On the following morning Sammy rode back toward the ranch, but he consumed three times three days for the return journey. He even had the hope that by the time he arrived, the swift-riding Mariscal might have arrived at his destination and brushed the outlaw into the other world. He even hoped that by the time he arrived, all would be over except the very marriage itself. For there could be no doubt that Kathleen would love the big man with all her heart the instant she laid her eyes upon him. How else could it be when he was a picture which so satisfactorily filled the eye? But Sammy Green, as he pushed his horse slowly over the range and through the forests, blazed away steadily with the Colt at trees and rocks and squirrels—whatever he saw.

It was a vital necessity to learn how to handle the gun as soon as possible, for one of these days tidings would roll up out of his past and overtake him, tidings borne to the Burnside ranch which would tell the cowpunchers there that they had been afraid of a nobody all these days. And when that time came, then there would be a need for a gun. Sammy shuddered when he thought of it, and, when he shuddered, he shot straighter than ever.

In fact, every time he reached for the Colt it was not hard for him to imagine that he was even then fighting for his life, and every time his finger curled around the trigger it was not hard for him to conjure up the form of a furious cowpuncher twenty yards away.

He used to say to himself, as he fired, not—"That ends him!"—but—"At least I've died fighting . . . I've made him hear my bullet!" Yet it was melancholy work, this preparation for a battle in which he must lose. But, at least, his wrist no longer ached from the strain of wielding and firing the heavy revolver. And every time he touched the trigger he wished more profound good luck to Louis Mariscal.

In the meantime, another act was developing in the play which he had set on foot. He had not been long gone in one direction from the house of Mariscal, and Mariscal himself had gone in another direction, when a tall and slenderly made man with a carefully-combed mustache rode up to the door of the cabin. When he beat on the door, the old man whom Louis had left behind him as a caretaker came out to examine the stranger.

"Where," said the latter, "is Mariscal?"

"Gone."

"Where?"

"I dunno," said the old man.

"How long will he be gone away?"

"I dunno."

"Why did he leave?"

"I dunno."

"Did he sell his place?"

"I dunno."

"Why are you here, then?"

"To stay until he comes back."

Here the other sighed and wiped his forehead, as having passed through a most aggravating test.

"What trail did Louis hit?" he asked.

"I dunno."

"Did you see him start?"

"Yes."

"Which way did he seem to be going?"

"Seemed to be going off yonder." And the old man pointed to the northeast.

"If he comes back before me," said the young fellow, turning the head of his horse in the designated direction, "just tell him that Harry Link is looking for him and looking hard!"

With this he cantered his horse away and kept on steadily for half a mile until he emerged from the section where the hoof prints of cows and horses were inextricably tangled, coming down to water. He passed this section, and, presently, he found beyond it a solitary trail of a horse. It was not hard to discover that it was a ridden horse and not a wandering animal. It kept a little too straight, and, though it was not traveling fast as the distance it stepped at a trot indicated, yet it was not tempted to one side or another by the most succulent and inviting heads of grass. So, deciding that it must be the trail of Louis Mariscal, he stuck steadily to it.

No doubt he would have overtaken the other before noon, for his horse was a stronger traveler and he was far lighter than Mariscal, but in the middle of the morning his horse developed a touch of lameness that made him make an exchange at the first ranch he reached. Then, far more poorly mounted than before, he struck ahead.

His first impulse when he started down the trail had been to accuse Mariscal of fleeing from him, having learned his purpose of finally settling the question of supremacy which existed between them. For Harry Link was one of those who are born to be fighters. If all is well, and they have sufficient opportunities to risk their necks in order to break the necks of others, they remain peaceful citizens, serving as sheriffs, or deputies, and crowding into the forefront of posses. Such was Harry Link.

If times became too dull and quiet, the great danger was that such men would start out to hunt up a little excitement on their own responsibility. And the result of such an expedition could only be a break between the adventurer and the law. And such, again, was Harry Link. His slender fingers loved to wrap themselves around the butt of a gun and launch destruction at the breast of another. He was not a bully, to be sure; but he was constantly on the hunt for someone who would give him an even battle. In that mood it had been that he approached Samuel Green and beat him. In that mood he was now on the trail of Louis Mariscal. For he need fear no reprisal on the part of the law, if he disposed of such a warrior as Louis. That Mariscal had given up his wild ways and settled down to the sober life of a rancher was something that the world had not yet come to appreciate.

So Harry stuck like a ferret to the trail. Indeed, there was something of the weasel even in the physical appearance of the man with his little head, his long, narrow body, and his tiny, glittering eyes. He seemed perpetually about to make some astonishing discovery, so brilliant were his eyes, as though with expectation. And the next morning, rising with the first upward springing of the light in the eastern sky, he pushed ahead so fast that, when the sun actually rose, he had come upon the camp of Mariscal. He left his horse behind him among the trees, scurried forward, and watched the larger man for some time from behind a tree.

It was fascinating work to Harry Link. He had never before seen the big man, but he had heard him so often and so thoroughly described that he felt that he knew him at the first glance. Finally he stepped out from behind the tree, already certain of victory in his bloodthirsty heart, already feeling that this was the chief of all his victims.

He stood for a full five minutes with his back leaning against a tree, watching, while Louis finished his breakfast. And he enjoyed hugely the contortions of the other, as the quiet eyes bored into his back. Sometimes he shrugged his shoulders violently. Sometimes he shivered all over. Sometimes he raised his head and sat perfectly still. Once he swung his head around and looked straight behind him at the watcher, but, as often happens when one remains still, the observer was unmarked.

Finally he glided forth and laid a hand on the shoulder of the big man, and the latter whirled to his feet with a shout of astonishment. He recognized Link instantly, though he had never laid eyes on him before. Plainly he had dwelt on descriptions of his rival as much as the latter had done on descriptions of him.

"Harry Link!" he cried.

"Come a long ways to visit you, Louis."

They shook hands.

"Sit down and have breakfast with me," said Mariscal.

"I can't do that."

"Why not?"

"I got a superstition about that."

"Don't understand you, Link."

"In my family they say that it's bad luck to sit down to the table and eat with a gent that you figure on killing later on, Mariscal."

After this a little silence fell between them. Louis Mariscal had turned white, but his eyes did not weaken from the gaze of his enemy. Instead, the hard muscles at the roots of his jaw began to bulge.

"You've come trouble hunting," he said at last.

"That's me."

"I guess I'm the man to give you what you want then, Link. Guns, or knives, or hands, I'm ready for you!"

Harry Link, however, now sat down upon a fallen log and

regarded his companion with the greatest calm and pleasure.

"There ain't any hurry about this little party," he declared. "I'd as soon finish you at noon as now."

"You're sure of yourself, Link."

"Very sure."

"I'm just as sure for my part. I'll tell you where your grave will be, Harry. I'll roll away that log you're sitting on and push it over the hole, yonder. That'll do to cover you up, so's the wolves can't get at you."

"Thanks," said Harry Link. "I'm glad of that hint. I'll do the same by you."

"You ain't man enough. You couldn't budge that log."

Harry flushed with anger. "I guess I ain't going to be able to wait till noon," he said.

"It's a fine day, Link. Never seen a better day. Why not stay around and enjoy things as long as you can?"

"I can't put off the party too long. I'm figuring right now where you'd die the best . . . head or the heart, Mariscal. But I'd rather hate to spoil that fine face of yours."

"Thanks," said Mariscal. "I won't worry so much about yours. I'm ready when you are, son."

"No hurry . . . no hurry!"

"If you talk so big right now, tell me why you run away when you heard how I was coming to get you?"

"Run away?"

"What else was it? I don't mind telling you. I'm riding to get the girl I'm going to marry."

"She'll wait a tolerable long time before she sees you, then."

"I ain't so sure of that. After I get married, it ain't likely that she'll want me to chase around gunning. I got to make the best of the few times that are left to me. I wish there was two of you, Harry, so's you'd stretch out longer. But still you're better'n nothing."

"Marrying!" murmured the smaller man. "Well, somehow I never figured that you'd be the marrying kind. *I* ain't, for instance. I wouldn't have a girl depending on me . . . not with the kind of a life that I'm leading. And I wouldn't see a gent like you undertaking to support a woman when you know well that you ain't going to stick to the job.''

"Thanks for them thoughts,'' said Louis. "Take a whirl at marrying this girl yourself. To get her, all you got to do is to get rid of Maurie Washburn.''

"Eh?''

"Does he sound as big as that to you?''

"Oh, he ain't any more to me than any man is. What are *you* aiming to do with Maurie?''

"Take him alive,'' said Louis Mariscal, "and then I'll bring him down and turn him over to the sheriff. After that, I'll tell them where to find your grave, and, while they're looking for it, I'll go to get the girl.''

"You're talking crazy, Louis.''

"I'm telling you the facts.''

"What has Washburn got to do with any girl?''

Briefly Louis detailed the story of the hounded rancher, his rage and despair, and the fashion in which he had offered to give his daughter in marriage to any man who should kill the outlaw.

"So you started for him?'' said Harry.

"Why not?''

"You don't look like a fool to me. I'll tell you why not, if you don't know . . . it's because there ain't no man in the mountains that could stand up to Washburn with a gun or any other sort of a weapon. He's a devil when it comes to a fight! The girl will sure never be married so long as she waits for Washburn to be taken or killed.''

He shook his head with such solemnity that even Louis Mariscal was daunted. He remained in silence for a time and then remarked: "What would *you* do in front of Washburn?''

"Run,'' said the other frankly.

"The devil!''

"So would you.''

"Link, I got an idea."

"If it's about a way of getting rid of Washburn, it ain't any good."

"This girl has a fortune besides her good looks."

"That's right. I've heard of the Burnside ranch."

"Suppose that the two of us got at Maurie Washburn and got rid of him. Then we could fight it out to see which of us should claim the right to marry the girl."

"That's an idea, Mariscal, that's good enough to have come out of the dictionary."

And they wrung each other's hand.

"Can I trust you, Harry?"

"To the limit, old son!"

"Then let's lay out a plan of campaign. It's going to take hard planning to get at Washburn, two to one. He'll fight anybody that goes alone on his trail, but he'll be a fox we got to corner before the two of us can get a crack at him!"

Chapter Seven

"Maurie Washburn"

The most famous marauders who have written their red names into the history of the West have been men more terrible in mentality than in body. They have been captains of battle with the minds that love destruction and the wits to bring destruction about.

But Maurie Washburn was the great exception. He united the two qualities of physical and mental prowess. He was designed by the Creator as a destroying plague. In size he was not a giant by any means. He was perhaps a shade under six feet in height, and his weight was not more than two hundred pounds. But those pounds consisted of bone and rubbery muscle only. Those muscles of his seemed threefold stronger than the muscles of ordinary men. There was a difference as great as that which exists in the muscles of a horse. For there are all manner of differences in power. Imagine a house cat increased, without loss of vital vigor, to the dimensions of a bull terrier. What two dogs in all the world could for an instant stand up before her razor-sharp claws or her needle teeth? She could rip out the heart of a wolfhound with one sweep of her claws. Or imagine the muscular little terrier increased without loss of comparative power to the size of a Great Dane? He could outpull a horse!

And so it was with Maurie Washburn. He had the muscles that make a little man formidable among giants. And with that perfect quality he combined size, also. So that Washburn in action with his hands was like a great whirlwind. He seized and smashed things with the same gesture.

His face was marked with the characteristics of resistless might. His head was proudly borne on a mighty column of a neck. His eyes were ordinarily dull, as though there was little in the world worthy of bringing the light of excitement into them. And between his eyes there was a perpendicular furrow like the wrinkle between the eyes of a lion. Even without weapons he would have been more formidable than a wild beast, but, combining with his physical prowess an uncanny adroitness in the use of guns, he was like a destroying angel through the cattle ranges in the mountains.

This was the man who sat, or rather lay at his ease, before the fire in the house of John Watkins. It was John's own chair, but when Maurie Washburn arrived it was given over to the great marauder. It was his right, as was everything else in the house, for Maurie was from of old the benefactor of the poor squatter.

For five years it was the money of Maurie Washburn that had carried the farmer through his seasons of sickness, bought clothes and food for his wife and children, and on the whole made existence possible and pushed destruction away. In return, Washburn found in the house an unfaltering loyalty and a refuge that was almost conveniently located for him.

It was on a ridge, commanding a wide prospect east and west, that the foolish little farmer had built his house, but the folly that had made him build in such a location gave the outlaw just the outlook he needed. To Washburn the house was like a nest high on the mast of a ship. It enabled him to peer far off across the dark mountains and spy out the dangers as they came.

On this evening he dozed before the fire, his body slumped into the chair, his legs spread wide, his great hands dangling over the arms of the chair toward the floor, his head pulled over to one side and rolling upon his shoulder, as though his neck were broken. There he rested with mouth half open, his snoring regular and loud. At one end of the room the father of the family brooded over a time-yellowed newspaper. At another end the mother of the family worked frantically with needle and thread and patches to repair some of the damage that wear and tear had accomplished, and which the Monday washing had revealed. From time to time she looked up to her children with a hunted expression and parted her lips to speak, but, each time, she seemed to decide that it was better to use all of her energy in the work of repair rather than expend a single scruple of it in the effort of complaining.

As for the children, the two youngest wallowed in a corner, and the two eldest boys scrimmaged back and forth across the floor until the shoulder of one of them struck the edge of the table and the blow started the lamp quivering, so that it set up a peculiar metal shiver of sound. Instantly the head of Maurie Washburn was raised from his shoulder.

There was no yawning, no blinking, no stretching. He simply raised his head, opened his eyes, and was prepared to fight for his life, if need be, like a wild puma that has been cornered. Presently, he turned his head and watched the two elder boys who were scuffling.

"Billy," he said.

The boys stopped scuffling. The two younger children stopped wallowing in the corner. Mr. Watkins lifted his head from the paper. Mrs. Watkins shrank deeper into her chair and listened.

"Billy, what you running after Tom all the time for?"

"I got to do something, don't I? I can't just be sitting around all the day doing nothing, can I?"

The bandit regarded the child solemnly. Then he turned his glance to Tom, who was much smaller and whose bowed shoulders and pinched face told that he was suffering from some mortal disease.

"That's your way of playing a game, is it?" he asked.

"Ain't that a good way? How do *you* play?" countered Billy.

"I got to fight, now and then," said the outlaw, "just to make a living."

"I got to fight, now and then," mocked Billy, "so's to have some fun."

"Go on then," said Maurie Washburn, "have your fun . . . but don't corner Tommy, or something is pretty liable to happen."

"Him!" scoffed Billy. "But what could *he* do?" He extended a scornful finger at Tom, and Tom shrank from his persecutor.

"I got to tell you this," said Maurie Washburn, "that I ain't afraid of none of the gents that come a-hunting me. I ain't afraid of none of them, no matter how soft and quiet and sneaking they come up to me."

He had lowered his voice to give vividness to his words, and his extended hand and ominous eyes so well imitated the stalking beast that Mrs. Watkins gasped and dropped her thimble.

"I don't care nothing about them that tackle me, even from the rear," said the outlaw. "What I'm afraid of is some dog-gone coward that may get cornered and start fighting back one of these days."

"Why?" asked Billy.

"Because when a coward, or a gent that thinks he's a

coward, gets to fighting, he's apt to make more fur fly than ten of them that make fighting a regular sort of a profession. Understand?''

''I don't,'' said Billy.

''Wait till you've pestered Tommy a little while longer, and maybe you'll get your eyes opened!''

Billy studied the big man for a silent time. Then he advanced cautiously on Tommy again. And Tommy, as always, whined and retreated toward his mother. And his mother gathered him within her sheltering arm and shook her head with a silent frown at Billy—a silent frown, for the outlaw was already sinking back into his sleep, and he must not be disturbed. Sometimes they had known him to stay about the house for ten days, but hardly awake for a longer time than was required in the eating of his meals. His capacity for sleep was endless, and yet they knew that his capacity for wakefulness was also endless. Tradition told many tales of how he had remained on watch for days at a stretch.

After a few moments Tommy strayed away from the sheltering arm of his mother again, and, the instant he was gone, Billy dove in between him and protection and began a steady attack. In fact, he was spurred on by curiosity. He wanted to do exactly what the outlaw had warned him against, and, when he had cornered his brother, he would see what happened.

What happened was that Tommy, when the wall fenced him in close on two sides, simply wound his arms around his head and began to blubber. And Billy was about to turn to the bandit and call his attention to his false prophecy, giving one more cuff.

It landed by chance, rather than by design, upon the exposed ear of Tommy, and that ear had already been so thoroughly pummeled that all the nerves in it were jumping. The swinging cuff landed. There was a yell of pain and rage from Tommy, and he struck out with a clenched fist.

No doubt luck stood on the side of Tommy for the fist,

that had been blindly driven, landed flush on the jaw of his brother, and Billy's shoulder struck the floor. Before he could rise, little Tommy had him by the hair and was whacking his head against the boards.

The screams of Billy pierced the roof. Finally, Tommy was dragged away by the strong hand of his father, who deposited him across his knee and prepared to spank him. But the suspended hand did not fall. Maurie Washburn had not turned in his chair. He had been dreaming before the fire with a smile, as of one who finds happy thoughts before him. But now he spoke, as though he had been watching every movement of the late struggle.

"Let the kid alone, Watkins."

The hand of Watkins remained suspended in air at the voice of his patron.

"He was near to murdering Billy," he complained.

"Billy sure needed a lesson," said Washburn. "I told him what would happen if he cornered Tommy, and it happened. That's all there is to it. Let Tommy alone."

So Tommy was deposited upon the floor, and there he stood straight and proud of his victory.

"That's what happens when a gent gets cornered," said the outlaw. "Weak man will fight like a snake when there ain't no way out except by fighting. He puts all of his scare into his fists. You see?"

And he turned with a grin to Billy, who was still blubbering, more in fright than in pain.

"I'm going to bed, and the rest of the tribe along with me," declared Watkins. "Time for kids to turn in. Early to bed and early. . . ."

"I got to finish this patch on Billy's shirt. He ain't got nothing clean to wear for tomorrow," said Mrs. Watkins. "I'll be right along."

The father and the four children disappeared, and, when

they were gone, Maurie Washburn turned in his chair and confronted the mother.

"Now," he said, "we can have that talk I been needing to have with you. To start at the beginning . . . how much did they pay you?"

Chapter Eight

"Treachery"

"I dunno," breathed Mrs. Watkins, hugging her sewing to her withered breast and looking at the outlaw as if he were a ghost. "I dunno what you mean?"

"I guess you know right enough. How much?"

"How much what?"

"Money."

She shook her head, but she could not speak.

"I ain't going to hurt you," said the big man. "I ain't a woman beater. I ain't even going to tell Watkins about it . . . not so long as you talk right out and tell me the whole thing."

"Maurie . . . ," she began.

"So long as you tell me the whole truth."

"God help me!"

"You ain't going to need no help. You can help yourself. How much did they pay you?"

"A hun . . . I mean . . . ," she began.

"They bought me off'n you for a hundred dollars, then!"

"No, no, no!"

"I never figured to be sold that cheap."

"I don't know what you mean, Mister Washburn!"

"I'll call your husband down. I figure that he'll be pretty interested in what you got to say, and maybe he'll know some better way of making you talk."

She shook her head. But when he rose to his feet and stepped toward the door, she cried out suddenly. So he turned and found that she had buried her face in her hands. He came back and stood behind her chair. His voice was wonderfully soothing and soft, but, now that she could not watch him, his face was demoniacal.

"Just think of me as a friend. Tell me everything. That's the best way out. They offered you a hundred. . . ."

"Oh, after all you've done for us. . . ."

"I ain't done so much," said Washburn. "Besides, you never could tell when I'd come to the end of my rope. And you been needing money pretty bad lately."

"That's it, Maurie. I been trying to find another way out of it all the time . . . but there didn't seem to be no other way. Then they come along and offered me that hundred dollars. They said that they had you anyways. That it didn't make any difference what I done, but that, if I helped a little, they'd give me the money."

"Stop crying. I tell you again, I ain't going to do you no harm! Just talk it all out. Then you'll feel a pile better."

"But I shouldn't say a word till I've give them back the coin that. . . ."

"You can give it back, and you'll get two hundred from me to take the place of that hundred. Understand?"

"You're a good man, Maurie. Oh, you're the best man in the world."

"That ain't true. The best man in the world ought to be worth a lot more than a hundred dollars to a friend."

"I was crazy when I did that thing. I didn't know what I was doing. Honest, I didn't, Maurie."

"When did they come to you?"

"Yesterday."

"When you went out in the morning?"

"How did you know that?"

"No matter how I knew. Why, you'd be surprised if you found out the half of what I know. I know enough to tell you when you're speaking the truth about this, and when you ain't. Go on . . . when you went out in the morning . . . ?"

"I'd picked up an armful of wood, and then I felt that somebody was standing there behind the shed watching me. I looked around right quick, and there I seen a tall young man standing . . . a mighty skinny and tall one, working at his mustache with one hand and his right hand on the butt of his revolver. It give me a terrible start, Maurie."

"I guess it did. Did he pull the revolver on you?"

"He stood back and didn't say nothing."

"I says . . . 'Good morning, mister. Might you be the new rancher come over from the ridge beside. . . .'

" 'I ain't a rancher, ma'am,' says he.

" 'Well,' says I, 'come in and have a snack with us.'

"So he ups and walks right to me and stands there, still rubbing at his whiskers and staring down at me.

" 'Maurie Washburn lives in that there house of yours,' he says to me.

"I felt like the ground had been yanked out from under my feet.

" 'Maurie Washburn?' says I. 'You don't mean the gent that's the great robber?'

" 'I mean just him,' says he. 'Will you confess?'

" 'I dunno him, except by hearing of the terrible things that he's done,' says I. 'Are you a sheriff or something?'

" 'That can wait for the trial,' says he. 'You'll find out who and what I am when I get you to the jail. You can tell the judge your story.'

"I dropped down on my knees.

" 'For mercy's sake, sir,' says I, 'I got four children.'

" 'It's thinking of the four children,' says he, 'that makes me want to give you a chance. But when you start right in with lying . . . why, that changes my mind a whole pile.' "

"He was a pretty clever one," murmured the outlaw. "But go on, Missus Watkins."

" 'What chance could you give me?' says I."

"You were a fool to say that!" snarled Washburn.

" 'I can give you a chance to do a fine thing for yourself and your husband and your kids,' says he. 'All you got to do is to act with us.'

" 'For what?' says I.

" 'For capturing Washburn,' says he.

" 'I'd rather die,' says I. 'Because there ain't a better or kinder man nowhere than this same Washburn that you. . . .' "

"You're lying now," broke in Maurie Washburn calmly.

"It was something like that that I said to him, anyway. And after he'd heard me, he says . . . 'That ain't going to mean much to the jury. They'll have to. . . .'

" 'D'you mean to arrest me?' says I.

" 'Right quick,' says he.

"I didn't know what to think or to do. I stood there twisting my hands together and waiting for a word to come, and then he says . . . 'You can't help Washburn, but you can help us. The way things stand, you go to jail, and your husband gets hung for standing in with a murderer.' "

"Did the hound say that?" growled Maurie.

"Aye, he said that, and with his eyes terrible bright and steady, like he sure knew what he was saying. And he said . . . 'Your husband gets hung for standing in with a murderer, and, if your children come to any good end, it won't be because they have a father and a mother to take care of them . . . their father bein' a gallows bird and their mother being in prison.'

"And when he said that, it seemed to me like my heart would've busted.

" 'What can I do to save my babies?' says I.

" 'A whole pile,' says he. 'You can save your babies and your husband and yourself by doing what we want you to do.' "

"Well?" queried Washburn. "What was that?"

"Ain't there a curse," moaned the wretched woman, "on the heads of them that betray others? How can I tell you what I promised them?"

"You could betray me to them," said Washburn, and his face swelled with a terrible anger, "but you can't betray them to me. Is that how it stands?"

"No, no! Won't you listen to me, Maurie?"

"I'm listening hard and fast! Tell me what you was to do for them?"

Suddenly she could endure his eyes no longer, and her face dropped into her hands. The rest that she spoke was barely a distinguishable murmur.

"When tonight come. . . ."

"Tonight?" asked Washburn like an echo, and his eyes were fire as he leaned toward her.

"I was to let them come in through the back door so soon as you was in bed. And I was to go to the back door and open it and let them walk right in, and then they was to. . . ."

"You she-devil!" snarled Maurie.

"God have mercy!" she moaned.

"Go on . . . what was they to do?"

"Go up to the room where you was sleeping."

"How many of them?"

"Only two."

"Two?" cried Washburn.

He started to his feet and began to walk up and down the room hurriedly.

"I've sunk down as low as that, have I? Two of 'em will come hunting me? Is that the way they look on me now?

There was a time when they would have thought that six men wasn't enough to handle me. And now they come with two . . . only two!''

He worked himself into a wilder and wilder fury as he spoke, but the greater grew his anger, the softer became his voice and the more cat-like his step until at last the latter made no sound. But his fingers never ceased stretching stiff and then jumping into the palm of the hand, as though they were catching things in the air and squashing them to death.

"Go to bed!" he said. "Go to bed! There ain't any need of you staying up here any longer. Go to bed . . . you hear me?"

"I hear you, Maurie," she murmured.

And she began to gather up her sewing in haste, her head bowed, quite unable to meet his eye even then. Presently she rose to her feet and swayed across the room. At the door she paused again, with her hand on the knob, her head fallen, apparently struggling with herself to turn back and speak again to him, but it was evidently too much for her strength of mind, for now she opened the door hastily and passed out from the room.

Chapter Nine

"Washburn Acts"

Now Maurie Washburn went back to the fire. He first put out the lamp that had been left for his comfort. Then he slumped back in his chair before the fire and listened to the steps of Mrs. Watkins mounting to the loft, where the little sleeping rooms were; behind him his great bunched shadow wavered on the wall.

He did not stir for ten minutes, except once to lift his head, as though to listen to a rising wind that was coming up out of the north and whistling at the chimney. But, finally, he stood up quickly and glided across the room, opened the door into the front hall, and leaped into the darkness.

He struck down with his weight a soft and yielding figure beside the front door. This he now seized, as it went limp, and dragged it back into the light of the fire. It was Mrs. Watkins, and she had not fainted, but her muscles had become paralyzed with dread. She lay in a heap near the fire, with her head propped so sharply up against the wall that it seemed her neck must break under the strain. Her long thin arms sprawled beside her, with the rough hands turned palms up. And she dwelt in a fascination of horror upon Maurie Washburn.

He had turned into the pure brute, striding up and down the room in the ecstasy of his rage that made him grin at her like a beast whenever his eyes fell upon her face. What was the struggle that went on in him, she could not tell. At first, she wondered if he were not pondering on the way to destroy her. And, after that, she decided that he was weighing the question as to whether or not she should live or die. She dared not stir, though her position was giving her torture that increased every instant. But she dared not move, for fear he would crush out her life with a stamp of his foot.

At length he stooped suddenly till his face was close to her, and she thought for an instant that it was the face of the lord of all demons.

"You was going out to them," said Maurie Washburn. "That was it. You was going out to warn them that I knew, and that tonight wouldn't be a good time for the trick to be turned. Was that it?"

"No," she managed to whisper.

He wound his fingers carefully, almost tenderly, into the mass of her gray hair. Then he jerked her to her feet, and the gesture seemed to transform him on the instant into a giant.

"Tell me true," he snarled, close to her ear.

"I wasn't."

"If you lie," said Maurie, "I'll. . . ."

"Oh," she murmured, "I couldn't let them come walking in like rats into a trap."

"It was a pile better that *I* should be the rat, eh?"

He laughed mirthlessly, his voice shuddering away to a silence again.

"You devil!" he said, when he could speak. "You murderess! I'd have had my throat split wide open, like a chopped tree, before the morning, if you'd have had your way about it!''

"No, no, Maurie!"

"Stop whining and listen to me saying something that's for your best good to hear."

"I'm listening."

"You was going out to tell them what had happened, and that I knew."

Her head had fallen back a little. She was staring straight up into his face, and her own was so white that it seemed a wonder the grisly flesh could be living.

"I was going out to tell 'em," she admitted in the voice of one hypnotized.

"Instead of doing that, you're going right back up to your bed."

"I'm going right back up to my bed, Maurie . . . and God bless you for lettin' me go."

"One more thing . . . if you leave your bedroom again and try to get downstairs. . . ."

"No, Maurie, I won't. I swear to you that I won't never do it."

"If you should do it, lemme tell you what I'd do!" He drew in his breath, as though the very thought gave him the most exquisite pleasure. "I'd put a match to this old shack and see you and Watkins and the four brats go up in smoke and come down in ashes. That's all that I'd do!"

She reeled. He seemed to bring her upright by a single glance.

"Now go up to your bed!"

She fumbled her way to the door; she fumbled her way out and up the stairs, and Maurie Washburn lay in his chair and listened, a smile on his face like the smile of a connoisseur when he hears the sweetest music. He still waited until the lights had been put out upstairs—he could tell that by the cessation of all sounds in the chamber—and then he rose and went to the rear door of the shack.

There must be more to the illusion than the mere opening of the kitchen door. So he took from the wall one of Mrs. Watkins's faded aprons, which was hanging there on a nail, and, when he opened the door with his left hand, with his right hand he held before the opening the light-colored dress. There was hardly time to draw it back again, so close did the two stand prepared for the signal.

"We're here," said a whisper, and a tall man pressed into the doorway. "We're here and ready. And here's the rest of the money to show you that we mean to play fair with you. Now show us the way up to his room."

"Great guns!" cried his companion, suddenly and half aloud.

He had seen something, guessed something. And Maurie Washburn delayed no longer. He struck with the butt of his revolver, and the man in the doorway was crushed to a flattened heap upon the floor. The second man drew a gun. Washburn could see the gleam of it in the dark. And he fired under that gleam, as the gun was raised, and he saw his second enemy drop. Then he called for lights, knowing the Watkins family was near at hand, having heard them scurry down the stairs during the commotion.

He who had fallen in the doorway was only stunned, and his scalp was torn by the force of the blow. He was a huge young fellow, with blond hair, a tawny mane of it. Beyond him in the dark, his undischarged revolver in his hand, lay the second assailant. There was a bullet hole in his breast, and his heart would never beat again.

Maurie Washburn chose to do no more work. He sent the children to bed. Then he commanded Watkins to go out and bury the body of the dead man, and poor Watkins, looking more like a hunted rat than ever, took a pick and shovel and departed. Then Maurie turned to the woman. She was blue skinned with dread and with horror.

"Here's the first part of what you've done," he said, "you she-Judas! You sold me for money, and then you sold 'em back to me for fear! That's all that you done! Women like you ain't good enough for hell. And you're going to get some of your payment right now. Hang that lantern on the wall."

She obeyed.

"Now go over there and get that rope."

Mutely she followed his directions.

"Now, kneel over yonder by the man on the floor."

With a tottering step she obeyed. He lolled in his chair and regarded her with perfect complacency. One might have thought that his mind was happily filled by the contemplation of a great and good act of benevolence.

"Now tie his hands behind his back."

She obeyed.

"Cut the shirt off his back."

It was done.

"Take this knife."

He opened the blade and flicked it toward her so dexterously that the point stuck into the wood close to her knees. She had to make two distinct efforts to draw it forth, so great was her weakness. Finally she succeeded and stared toward Washburn to wait for his command. And, as she kneeled there with the knife in her hand, her eyes roved past him to the stairway, where it dipped down into the darkness from the second story. Out of the darkness, very dimly, like a ghost face, she could make out the features of the irrepressible Billy, who had stolen down from his bed to see what was happening. But Mrs. Watkins barely understood what meaning the face had. It was like a painted thing and not a reality to her numbed brain.

Chapter Ten

"Sammy Decides"

Under a pine tree sat Sammy Green, making music on his harmonicon, and, when he blew hard, his face swelled and his big ears stood forth, and he looked for all the world like an overgrown elf, a gigantic brownie, but not a man. And when he drew in his breath and sucked in his cheeks, he looked astonishingly like a lost soul wandering by the shore of Lethe—a soul that had wandered for a thousand years.

So Sammy sat under the pine tree and made music that floated with a wail to the bunkhouse and brought the cowpunchers to the door to listen and make their remarks.

"I'd rather have a coyote howling right at my ear," said one.

"Some day I'm going to step in his face," said another.

"And why don't he get out and ride on the trail of Washburn?" said another. "If he's such a much, why don't he get out and ride? We've heard a pile of talk about him, but

69

we ain't seen him doing anything worth mentioning excepting the eating of his three squares a day!''

And the music floated up to the ranch house and there it greeted the ears of Burnside and his daughter, Kathleen, where they sat on the verandah.

"Curse that noise!" said the rancher.

"And yet it has a queer sort of a fascinating meaning," said Kathleen.

"Hmm," said her father.

"I could really sit here and listen to it for hours."

"I could go mad, listening to it for ten minutes longer!"

"Then why don't you ask him to stop?"

"Tell a man-killer that his music is driving me crazy? I don't carry enough life insurance to make that sort of a remark worthwhile, honey!"

"I don't believe he's so fierce."

"Don't you never doubt that none! He's got the look and the way of a bad one. I wouldn't trust him with a gun for a minute, if he's got his fighting dander up."

"Well . . . ," said Kathleen.

"Well what?"

"Nothing."

"A girl," said the father, "can say more fool things in a minute than a man can say in a year."

"Who is that?" asked Kathleen.

As she spoke, her father saw a horseman swinging down the trail that led from the low ridge into the valley and toward the ranch house. Yet he could not be seen distinctly. It was not light enough for that. It was that deceptive time of the evening when there is less light than one thinks, and when one will strain one's eyes vainly and long.

The horseman, however, was approaching at so rapid a gait that he was soon before them. And as he threw himself from his horse and came toward them, taking off his hat and waving it to Kathleen, they saw that it was Jerry Matthews from a neighboring ranch. Jerry was an old suitor. He had wooed Kathleen so long that it had become a habit with both of them. He would have counted the week lost in which he did not ask her to marry him, and she would have considered that week lived in vain in which she had not refused Jerry.

He sat on the railing of the verandah with his elbows on his knees, and talked to them both, with his eyes upon Mr. Burnside most of the time, but his keenest glances darted at Kathleen. For, of course, she was acting her part with her usual skill. She knew—how could she help but know?—that the golden mat at the back of her chair made a perfect background for her. She also knew that her profile was much the best angle from which to view her face. And, therefore, it was that she tossed one arm above her head and looked so languidly, so carelessly toward the darkening hills to the west. One might have thought that all of her heart was lost in the contemplation of their grave beauty. But, as a matter of fact, it was simply that, by turning her head in this fashion, her profile was presented to poor Jerry, and with the shimmering gold cloth in the background, she knew well enough that his heart must be leaping.

"Who's the musician?" asked Jerry.

"That's the gunfighter," said Burnside. "And if he wasn't a gunfighter, we wouldn't stand for his noise."

"I heard a noise up from away south," said Jerry, "that he wasn't no gunfighter at all, but a lazy bum."

"Jerry!" cried the girl.

"I can't help what I hear, can I?"

"I don't believe that you ever heard it! You're simply making that up, Jerry Matthews!"

"Honest Injun."

"There aren't any honest Injuns."

Which was enough to start them laughing, and, as the clear trill of the girl's laughter rippled through the thickening air of the dusk, the harmonicon stopped its drawling notes. At once the silence stepped more intimately about everyone; the whole of the outer night seemed to be listening to the conversation on the verandah. As a matter of fact, Jerry's loud young voice had enough of a ring to it to carry his words plainly to the bunkhouse and to the keen ears of the pseudo-gunfighter who sat under the pine tree.

"Matter of fact," said Burnside, muffling his voice, "I'm beginning to get impatient about Green. He's a great hand to sit still and do nothing. Maybe he's hatching his scheme for catching Maurie Washburn, but I can't help doubting it."

"Know what Maurie has done now?"

"Dunno. What next?"

"Couple of days back, along comes a gent into the town of Wascott over yonder. . . ."

"I know that place. That's where old Grafton lives that's got that outlaw hoss."

"That's the place. Well, along into Wascott in the early morning comes a gent with his hands tied behind him and his back all black with dried blood. He got into the middle of the street and dropped on his face. They got him into a house and give him a drink of whiskey. Then they washed the blood off'n his back, and this is what they seen carved right into the flesh . . . 'Washburn's work!' "

"Cut into the *flesh*," breathed Kathleen, half fainting with the horror of that thing.

"When he could talk, he told how it had happened . . . how him and another gent had tackled Washburn and got beaten . . . how Washburn made a man named Watkins, whose house he was staying in, bury Harry Link, who was shot dead, and how Washburn then made Missus Watkins take a knife and cut those letters into the back of Louis Mariscal."

So much of it had been listened to complacently enough by Sammy Green, but now he rose to his feet and rested a hand against the trunk of the pine tree to steady himself.

"And Mariscal came down into the town more dead than alive."

"The beast! The demon!" cried Kathleen. "Oh, who will rid the world of him?"

"There ain't any three men able to stand up to him," said Jerry Matthews calmly. "That's the facts, and we might as well face 'em. Nobody's ever been able to do nothing with him. We all know that, and we might just as well put the facts in a pipe and smoke 'em up. Ain't I right, Mister Burnside?"

"Seems like you are. But why should the devil have made a woman do his dirty work on Mariscal?"

"Seems that Mariscal had bribed her to let him get into her house and get at the outlaw in the middle of the night. Then Maurie Washburn got wind of something being up, made her confess, and . . . you know the rest."

Sammy Green could wait to hear no more. He cleaned the harmonicon with his usual care, then he wrapped it in a silk handkerchief, and went into the bunkhouse. There he sat and gave the big Colt revolver the most careful cleaning it had ever received.

"Looks like you got a job on hand," said one of the men to Sammy.

He could not resist the temptation. "Nothing much," he said. "Just a little job of getting a gent that's been bothering a friend of mine."

"Who's been doing that?"

"Name is Washburn," said Sammy.

He shivered with apprehension at the very sound of the word. He wanted to stop. He wanted to keep from speaking the words that would drive him on. But the amazement on the face of the cowpuncher made it impossible for him to keep quiet.

"Maurie Washburn is the name," continued Sammy Green. "I'm going out to get Washburn, or else he's going to get me."

Chapter Eleven

"The Plan"

When in his dreams Sammy Green had seen himself standing face to face with the bandit and whipping his gun from the holster, he had always fired with a perfect nonchalance, and the battle always followed a trailing of Washburn that had been done without any sounding of trumpets. He had returned from the battle and carelessly mentioned, three days later, that he had done the work, and that the murderer was no more.

All of this was in his dreams. As a matter of fact, what he actually did was to go to Kathleen Burnside the next morning and draw her to one side.

"I've come to say good bye," said Sammy, trying to smile and only succeeding in making his lips tremble.

"You? Sammy Green, why are you going?"

He observed her a little vaguely. He had never been quite so close to her before, and it seemed to Sammy that her joyousness poured into him like a light and set him shivering with her presence. She was smaller than he had dreamed, looking from greater distances. Certainly she was shorter than he, for she was actually lifting her head a little in order to look him in the face.

"It's Washburn," he said huskily.

"Oh!"

"I've got to go."

"But you look white, Sammy!"

"Because . . . because I'm scared, Kathleen."

"Now you're joking. I know that you're one of those men who are never afraid."

"That's not true. I'm . . . I'm sort of sick inside."

"Then why do you go? Oh, Sammy!"

It was a wail in which he saw all her belief in him and his heroism melt away. And yet the imp of the perverse made him talk on and tell her the truth about himself.

"Because of you, Kathleen," he found himself saying rapidly. "Because I love you . . . because I can never have you . . . because I had a pile rather die trying to win you than to keep right on living and loving you and never. . . ."

He choked. Do heroes weep? And do they weep out of self-pity? Alas, that it should be said, but the great, bright tears had rushed up into the bright eyes of Sammy Green that were usually so coldly twinkling. He turned and rushed away to hide his emotion, galloped off into the woods.

What did Kathleen do and say? She cried out, then saw that he was gone, and ran straight to her father.

"Dad!" she cried.

"Well?" he said.

"Oh, Dad, what terrible thing do you think has happened?"

"I dunno. What?"

"Maurie Washburn. . . ."

"What of him?"

"Sammy Green has gone to kill him!"

"Sammy! God bless that boy!"

"But . . . don't you see . . . ?"

"What?"

"Nothing," whispered Kathleen softly, and turned away slowly.

And, in the meantime, Sammy Green rode straight across the mountains, pausing only to feed and rest his horse when it was absolutely necessary. He traveled, moreover, through a region where there were few houses, no telegraph or telephone wires, and over a region where it was very doubtful if any other person was riding half as hard and fast as he, and, yet, when he reached the town of Wascott, the news of his purpose in coming had preceded him by hours and hours. Everyone knew why he had come. Everyone was prepared to stare at him.

As for Sammy, he hardly cared whether he lived or died. He was only sure that he had disgraced himself forever in the eyes of Kathleen. Whenever he recalled what he had said, how his voice had trembled, and how at last—oh, misery!— the tears had actually rushed into his eyes. When he thought of these things, he bowed his head and was ready to perish, so long as he never had to face her again. Even the thought of her was an intolerable shame.

And shame is a mighty force. Shame will make a dog that crawled to the feet of his master for fear of a whip leap at his throat for fear of laughter. Shame will make ten regiments charge into the face of destruction, each running furiously lest some one man might be able to see ten thousand falter—ten thousand men afraid of the opinion of one. Such, however, is the might of shame. But in Sammy Green it was concentrated until his slender body was poured full of it. Sometimes he closed his eyes and turned white as he remembered just what had happened. And sometimes he actually went so far as to lay his hand on the butt of his revolver.

"But no," said Sammy Green, "I ain't got the courage

to do that. I ain't even got the courage to point a gun at myself.''

So he rode on until he came to the town of Wascott. He kept telling himself that he had better throw himself over a cliff than face death for a cause that was already lost. He had confessed to the girl that he was a coward. How could he undo that damage?

In the meantime, he had hardly time to think. He was besieged with admiration and questions. From the young children to the old men, everyone knew his face before he had been in town for two hours. What would he do? How would he go about catching the terrible outlaw? How could he expect to trail him successfully in a country with which he himself was not familiar?

''There ain't going to be any trouble,'' said Sammy Green. ''All I'm going to do is go out of town and camp in a shack that I passed coming up toward Wascott. And I'll just wait there till Washburn comes along, because I know that he's sure to come, sooner or later. He's near to the town. That's plain from the way that he sent in poor Mariscal.''

And when he spoke the name of Mariscal, a flush of anger and despair would tinge the cheeks of Sammy Green. For it seemed to him that worse than death had been inflicted upon the hero whom he had chosen beforehand as the husband of Kathleen. It was in vain that he told himself Louis was really unworthy, because he had attempted to buy the death of the outlaw through the treason of a woman. In spite of himself, he remembered the upright carriage and the fine, frank face of the other. And it seemed to him that Mariscal was dead, indeed, and only a ghost of his old self walked the earth.

''And then you'll wait for him to come? But why should he come?''

''Because he knows that the whole world is waiting to hear how his fight with me came out.''

''And you think that you got a chance, then?''

''I'm going to kill Washburn,'' Sammy would say with

perfect calmness. "The way he's done his killings has been to take folks by surprise and then shoot before they're looking. But I'm going up there to make him fight fair and square and take an even start with me."

"How can you do that?"

"By taking along a witness. That old gent that sits out yonder in front of the blacksmith shop . . . his hand shakes so much that he can't hardly handle his pipe without shaking all of the tobacco out of the bowl . . . I'll take him along. Washburn won't dare to murder a helpless old man like him. And he'll be the witness against Washburn, if Maurie takes me by surprise. I'm just going out to sit down in front of the old shack and wait for Washburn to come . . . and, when he hears how I'm waiting, and that he's got to step right out and take his chance, he'll sure begin to get sick to the stomach."

"And will he come?"

"What sort of a reputation will he have left if he don't come?"

Chapter Twelve

"The Victor"

It was exactly in this fashion that the historic combat took place. Old Noll Compton was taken by Sammy Green as his companion in the great adventure, and the old fellow went along like a hero marching forth to battle. As a matter of fact, he was as delighted as an old actor who is asked to come forth from retirement to take again an important rôle behind the footlights.

In the meantime, as the pair of them waited for the coming of the destroyer, they lived upon the fat of the land. For the good housewives of the town of Wascott vied with one another in baking pies and pastries and bringing them forth to the place where the hero awaited the foeman.

Sammy Green, however, barely touched the dainties. He left them to be devoured by his ancient companion, and that worthy showed an appetite and digestive power worthy of a Hercules. But, as for Sammy, he had passed into a long dream. He thought of nothing but Kathleen and strove to crowd into his mind all of the pictures of her that he had ever seen. He remembered her grave and smiling, talking with abandon and listening with eagerness, her head thrown back in a certain way that was to Sammy irresistibly lovely.

He hardly touched food. He even forgot his cigarettes. As the old man, who was his companion, afterward said: "Seemed like he was just concentrating on one thing every minute, all day and every day. Wouldn't hear me when I talked to him. Just sat there with his back to the wall and smiled at nothing."

The wait continued for exactly three days, and on the third day the crisis came. Maurie Washburn arrived. Sammy Green had always expected that he was going to dart suddenly out upon him, but, instead, he found one day that among the brown shadows under a neighboring pine tree there was another shadow, and that this shadow had a shape strangely like a man. And then he saw that it was a man, and he waved a greeting.

For answer there stepped from beneath the branches of the tree no other person than Maurie Washburn himself. There was no mistaking him, or that impression of immense strength which he so forcibly gave. But Sammy did not rise from the old log on which he sat with his hands folded on his lap. To his utter amazement he was not afraid. There was simply a great relief that the agony of waiting was ended. Tomorrow Kathleen would know that he had died—that he had died like a brave man, no matter how his words had sounded to her at their last meeting.

"Well," said Sammy, "here you are at last, and a mighty long time you took in coming, Washburn."

"Get your gun," said the outlaw. "I've taken my chances in coming down this far, and now I'm going to finish you up quick. Get your gun out, you fool, and I'll finish you *pronto*."

Sammy Green only smiled. He felt almost a kindliness for

the big man of the woods, and some of that kindness went into his smile. "You're afraid, then, Maurie?" he asked. "I knowed it would work that way. You'd start out brave as a lion, and then you'd get to thinking." And he began to laugh.

"What in thunder are you laughing at?" asked Maurie Washburn.

Sammy Green saw that the lips of the big man were white. He could hardly believe it, and yet there was the testimony of his eyes that could not be a lie. The great outlaw was turning paler every instant. He was afraid—yes, he was afraid of Sammy Green who had not courage enough to keep himself from a nickname. It was unspeakably delightful to Sammy, this knowledge that he was inspiring terror—even an instant before he died.

"Your gun, curse you!" cried Washburn.

"Fair play!" cautioned the old man who had come around the corner of the cabin, and now stood as stiff as a corpse. And very like a corpse he was, with his sallow, drawn face.

"Fair play . . . nothing!" gasped Washburn. "What you trying to do . . . hypnotize me, or something?"

"It's the fear of what's coming," said Sammy Green, peering intently at the face of the other. "That's what you can't stand, Maurie . . . that's what's making your knees begin to get weak."

"You lie!"

"When I drop this handkerchief, you both go for your guns," said the old man, and he raised the handkerchief in his hand.

"Sure," said Sammy. "I'm ready whenever Washburn is. But you better wait till he gets over being so nervous. You see how he's shaking, partner."

"I'll blow you in two!" cried the big man.

But Sammy did not even look toward the fluttering handkerchief. No use for him to match his speed against the lightning skill of the outlaw. Instead, he leaned back and calmly watched Washburn.

"Take a last look around . . . that blue sky you'll never see again, Washburn."

"You little rat!"

"Some rats kill snakes."

"You, there . . . drop that handkerchief! Get this over with!"

"Quickly!" said Sammy, and marveled to find that he could be smiling as he spoke. "My friend Washburn is losing his nerve rapidly . . . rapidly."

With an angry outburst Maurie Washburn reached for his gun. From the corner of his eye Sammy Green saw that the handkerchief had not dropped, but, as the big man reached and whipped out his weapon, Sammy followed suit. But how slowly, how stiffly in comparison were his motions. He had barely laid hold of the butt of the gun when he was struck a crushing blow on the shoulder—the left shoulder—driving him back against the wall of the shack, while the roar of Washburn's gun sounded in his ear.

As he slipped down to the ground, he tugged out his gun and aimed it. He was wondering all the time that he was not more frightened. He was telling himself that he must act quickly before the wave of the death agony overtook him. He must die, fighting like a man, for the sake of Kathleen.

Again the gun barked in the hand of Washburn, and again the bullet struck. But they were not centered shots. The shaking fingers of the outlaw were telling in the favor of Sammy Green. And so, as the figure of Washburn grew dim before him, he pulled the trigger.

What Sammy heard next was the voice of a deep-throated man speaking in an adjoining room.

"That's the way a Green would fight to the last . . . even when a treacherous scoundrel had betrayed him . . . a Green would fight like that and kill his man, just as my Sammy did. I was always proud of that boy. I always expected great things from him.''

Could that be his father? He opened his eyes and looked up. The voice ran on in the next room, but over him leaned the tender face of Kathleen. He had only the strength to reach partly up to her. Then she was on her knees beside him.

''My hero!'' said Kathleen.

''Hush! Hush!'' said Sammy. ''It was all a mistake. I'm just a lucky gent.''

ACKNOWLEDGMENTS

"Little Sammy Green" under the byline Max Brand first appeared in Street & Smith's *Western Story Magazine* (6/30/23). Copyright © 1923 by Street & Smith Publications, Inc. Copyright © renewed 1951 by Dorothy Faust. Copyright © 1997 by Jane Faust Easton and Adriana Faust Bianchi for restored material. Acknowledgment is made to Condé Nast Publications, Inc., for their cooperation.

"Black Sheep" under the byline George Owen Baxter first appeared in Street & Smith's *Western Story Magazine* (7/28/23). Copyright © 1923 by Street & Smith Publications, Inc. Copyright © renewed 1951 by Dorothy Faust. Copyright © 1997 by Jane Faust Easton and Adriana Faust Bianchi for restored material. Acknowledgment is made to Condé Nast Publications, Inc., for their cooperation.

"Safety McTee" under the byline Max Brand first appeared in Street & Smith's *Western Story Magazine* (8/15/23). Copyright © 1923 by Street & Smith Publications, Inc. Copyright © renewed 1951 by Dorothy Faust. Copyright © 1997 by Jane Faust Easton and Adriana Faust Bianchi for restored material. Acknowledgment is made to Condé Nast Publications, Inc., for their cooperation.

BLACK SHEEP

Frederick Faust was unable to write plot-based formulary fiction. This short novel, which was first published in Street & Smith's *Western Story Magazine* (7/28/23), is character driven, and it is perhaps most significant that the protagonist, Faust's winged warrior, is a nine-year-old girl, Mary Valentine.

Chapter One

"Mary"

The barb of the cactus goes easily in, but it is difficult to get out. The minister was fond of saying that the thorn resembled sin, so easy in the commission, with consequences which clung so like a part of the flesh. It was about the minister, his thin face, his puckered mouth, his pale and enthusiastic eyes, that Mary Valentine was thinking, as she sat upon the ground and regarded the root of the thorn that was buried in her flesh. The intensity of the sting was like an ache, and yet it was some time before she could summon the courage to seize the little dagger and pluck it forth with an involuntary cry. She regarded the crimson point for an instant and then flung it from her in loathing, just as the minister said one should fling away temptation.

After that, she took hold on the flesh near the wound and pressed out a generous drop of blood, for her mother, years before, had told her that it was good to make a new cut bleed in order to wash out the poison. Finally, she stood up and tried her weight on the bare foot. And, though she had to turn the foot far to one side for a while, in ten steps she was walking as boldly and freely as ever, and the dust was squirting up between her toes. To be sure, every step hurt her, but even at the age of nine Mary Valentine had come to realize that pain is the commonest portion in the world. And since she stepped out bravely and freely, all in a moment the bleeding had ended, and the hot dust had burned away the sense of pain, so that her breath was no longer shortened, and she walked erect again.

She was as straight, as supple, and as strong as a boy; she had a boy's leanness of face, and the windy bits of sun-faded hair, that blew about it, made her seem only wilder and not more feminine. Yet somewhere the girl had to show forth, and, though boys might possibly have feet and hands so slim and small, certainly no boy since the beginning of time ever had knees so delicately and so truly made. They were exposed now because she had been in wading, and her overalls had been turned up. But for that matter, her legs were as tough a brown as the brown of her hands or her feet. She had been weathered and burned to a single rich tan, from head to foot, by the sun of the swimming pool.

Such was Mary Valentine as she came up from the creek, vaulted over half a dozen fences, which framed the corrals at the back of her uncle's house, and finally stood just inside the door of the kitchen. Uncle Marsh Valentine had tilted his chair back against the wall. All night he had been sitting at the table, facing his two sons, and all night the deep voices of the sons had rumbled on. To Mary, in the upper story of the old building, it had seemed like a strong murmuring of storm far away, and half a dozen times she had wakened and listened and then turned in her bed and fallen asleep once more, lulled by that rumbling of words. It was three years since Jack and Oliver had fled, when they were charged with the Dinsmore killing. And since the confession of a dying criminal in the state prison had freed them of that charge, they were but just returned, and naturally there was much for them to talk over with their father. They had talked since late in the evening. It was now mid-morning. But still their themes seemed as inexhaustible as the five-gallon jug of moonshine from which they poured their drinks now and again, for they disdained a pitcher. Jack was filling the glass of his brother, Oliver, at that moment. He picked the heavy jug up with one hand and then, with a mere twist of the wrist, rolled it over his arm and tilted a thin stream into the glass. They had been drinking and talking all night, and yet their hands were as strong and steady and their eyes as bright as when that conference began. Mary Valentine would have sold the hopes of the next ten years of her life, if she could have enjoyed the privilege of hearing one of the stories that these big and fierce men must have brought home.

They were more attractive than her uncle. For great physical strength and native fierceness of disposition in an older man is merely terrible, whereas in a youth it is both awful and beautiful. In sheer bulk of might, Marsh Valentine was still probably not far behind either of his boys, for time seemed to have seasoned and hardened him more than it weakened, and every one of the three were born strong without paying any price of labor or even of exercise. They were all of a height. How many inches they were above six feet Mary Valentine did not exactly know. They were all of a weight, yet she had not the slightest idea how many pounds they weighed. She only knew that other men walked with ease through the narrow front door of the Valentine house, but that her uncle and his two sons brushed the jamb on either side with their spread of shoulders.

But the shining black hair of Marsh Valentine was now turning gray, and the piercing black eyes were shadowed by steeply overhanging brows, and the throat of the man had thickened to a neck like that of a wild boar. He seemed stodgier and less active than his boys, moreover. And though they were not a hairbreadth taller than he, they seemed to have an advantage of inches. They might have stood for the young Hercules, but he was the very spirit of the older, with the shadow of doom already falling upon him, one might have said.

He faced Mary at the table now, and it seemed to her that he had been drinking at the fountain of youth in listening to the tales of his sons' exploits. What those adventures had been, Mary herself had heard at second-hand through the rumors of one kind and another that had often floated through the village. Those rumors related how the two had gone abroad among the mountains and had done many a wicked and many a cruel deed. But all had been forgiven by the governor, who declared that the false accusation had driven these two away from their home and fairly forced them into careers of crime. Mary Valentine, watching them from the doorway, did not know whether to think them more formidable or more glorious, so handsome, so huge, so fearless were they. Suddenly they spied her, for she had been sent to bed before their arrival the night before, since Uncle Marsh could not be bothered by the "brat" when his two boys came home for their first evening.

"Well, by guns," roared Jack Valentine, "if it ain't Mary!"

"Mary all growed up and looking more tomboy than ever!" thundered Oliver. "Come here, kid!"

Mary would have desired nothing better than to sit on his broad knee and hear strange stories of a thousand things about which she yearned to ask. But, when she glanced at her uncle, she saw instantly by his dark brow that he was not ready for an interruption. So she skirmished from a distance, to try out the enemy's disposition.

"I can't stay," said Mary.

"The dickens you can't!"

"Why not?" bellowed Oliver.

"Because Uncle Marsh doesn't want me to."

"He ain't said a word."

"But he's looking a whole heap of 'em."

"Come on, kid, and don't start trying to read Dad's mind. Come here and sit on my knee. I got something here to. . . ."

She looked at Uncle Marsh. He was staring down at the floor, apparently lost in thought, and, therefore, she decided that he was harmless, so she advanced with caution toward Oliver. She had almost reached him when a hand flicked out, like the lightning flip of a grizzly's forepaw, and knocked her head over heels back to the door through which she had just stepped.

"You've killed her!" shouted Oliver.

"Her head's busted!" began Jack, glaring at his father in horror.

And they both rushed to lift that slender little motionless body that now lay on the floor. But the sudden thunder of their father's voice stopped them in their tracks.

"Who's raisin' that kid?" he roared at them.

They turned upon him, growling.

"You'd like to have killed her, hitting her that hard," said Oliver.

"If I do the killing, I'll do the hanging," said the father, "and I'll take no back talk from a spindle-legged, wall-eyed, rattle-headed, half-growed-up pup like you. Keep your hands out of this little business, both of you!"

They stared at one another, their color rising, their eyes fierce, for they had been away from the parental roof for many a month, and their spirit of independence had swelled great in them. Yet the old habit of obedience conquered them—that and the fierce glare of Marsh Valentine, as he confronted them, so that he seemed in his chair bigger and more formidable than they appeared standing straight. They slunk back into their seats, and, as they did so, Mary recovered her senses and came staggering to her feet. As a matter of fact, there had been more accidental than intentional violence in the blow that felled her. Uncle Marsh had struck her many times, and heavily. But this morning he misgauged the weight of his hand and the strength of his wrist and the lightness of her slender little body. The cuff fell like the stroke of a bear's paw, and he had winced as he saw her fall. Yet, having done the thing, he determined to bluster it through, which is typical of all undisciplined natures.

She drew herself up, clinging to the side of the door. And the faces of Jack and Oliver burned with shame that they should have sat by and watched such a thing. Yet they thrust out their jaws and determined that they should not lose face. She stood by the door now, swaying a little and blinking. But she uttered not a word of complaint, and presently her eyes cleared.

Then Uncle Marsh said: "Mary, if you knowed that I wanted you not to come in, why the devil didn't you keep out?"

He spoke as kindly as he could, though even at the best his voice was rough. But Mary merely watched him for an instant, saying nothing, but fumbling on the kitchen table, that stood beside the door, until her hand had closed upon a heavy tumbler. This she suddenly threw, and not with an awkward and wobbling arm, as most girls throw, but whipping her hand over her shoulder in true boy fashion. With an upflung arm, Uncle Marsh barely avoided the flying peril. Otherwise, his forehead would have shattered the glass that now crashed upon the floor as Uncle Marsh lurched forward.

Mary, however, was gone through the door with the speed of the cracker on the end of the lash of a four-horse whip. And Uncle Marsh paused at the door to threaten her with an upraised hand and a word of thunder that went pealing away among the barns and the sheds.

"Why don't you catch her?" asked Oliver, as their father turned back into the room.

"Why don't I catch a swallow!" grumbled the big man and sat down again.

Chapter Two

"A Man with a Colt"

Mary sauntered on until she stood in the street, squirting the dust through the interstices between her toes by a dexterous movement of which she alone was master, and which was the passionate envy of every boy in the village. The twisting street was the intolerable white of molten steel; the reflection from it was almost as withering as the direct blast from the face of the sun, but Mary Valentine made a sufficient shade for her eyes by jerking down over them the brim of her black felt hat. At least, it had at one time been black, but was now a rich and ripening green.

To another that sun-beaten line of houses would have been blasted by monotonous familiarity, but not so with Mary Valentine. There was not a fence or a front gate, there was not a porch or a pane of glass, that did not call up some worthy recollection to her mind. Yonder was the steeple of the church, upon the hot top of whose stove she had dropped the cat and rent the singing of the choir in twain with a burst of superlative caterwauling. Yonder was the fence over which she had leaped in time to escape the snaky lariat of Deputy Sheriff Walters. And there was the big bay window of Judge Tompson's house that, with a well-aimed stone, she had shattered to bits.

Uncle Marsh had had to pay for that, and he had flogged her in such ample recompense that her flesh burned deep at the very memory. The thought spurred her on down the street. Under the cluster of willows around the corner she found the two Davis boys and Chet Smith, with Chet's little cousin.

"Hello, Skinny," said Sam Davis.

"Hello, Four-eyes," greeted Mary Valentine.

Her smile was perfectly nonchalant, but she stole a glance down at her legs. It was perfectly true that she was more slenderly made than the boys. It had irked her more than once. They had a burly mass of bone and brawn against which she could not stand, if she were cornered. But in the open, where activity counted, the matter was entirely different.

"I ain't wore glasses for a month," said Sam in stout defense.

"You got a batty look to your eyes, just the same."

"It's a lie," said Sam. "Ain't it, Chet?"

"Hello, Chet," said Mary gaily. "How you been feeling since Hal McCormack licked you?"

"He didn't lick me," said Chet, pale with shame and anger. "I just stumbled, and, when I fell, I hit. . . ."

"There was some that said when your nose began to bleed you just started bawling and run for home," remarked Mary.

"Do you believe that sort of a . . . ?"

"I dunno," said Mary, "you don't look like much to me."

Chet was speechless. Mary was famous for the cruelty of her tongue, but this was simply outrageous. How could Chet

95

know of the undeserved blow that had fallen upon her at her uncle's house?

"Let's take her down to the creek and duck her!" he cried at last. "Let's teach her a little politeness!"

The Davis boys had been victimized a hundred times by the vixen. They uttered a wild whoop of joy and threw themselves at Mary. How it happened, none of them could exactly tell, but their hands missed her. She stooped under the sweeping arms of the Davis boys as they closed on her. She rose with a handful of sand and blinding dust which she threw full into the face of Chet and, then, because her retreat was cut off by a barbed-wire fence on the one side and by the Davis boys on the other, she went up a big willow, like a cat, and sat in the branches, laughing at Chet Smith who was still coughing dust out of his lungs and wiping it out of his eyes. When he was able to speak, he called hoarsely to the Davis boys to help him rout the enemy from the stronghold, and the three plunged up among the branches.

But, alas, they had not counted upon their host. From capacious pockets she brought out rough-edged rocks, not pretty pebbles picked up at the creek, but jagged missiles meant for warfare. Then she wrapped her legs around the branch on which she was sitting and swung to the side with both hands free. Never were better targets; never was better marksmanship! Her first shot landed on the head of Sam Davis. Had it been centered a bit more, it would have knocked him out of the tree, but, as it was, it glanced off and merely raised a bump and a yell from him. Her second shot, aimed fairly for the face of Chet, was intercepted by his raised arm that was cut by the sharp edge of the stone, and the pain caused him to lose his grip. The result was that he slipped down through the branches with a scream of fear and, having managed to clutch a lower limb in time to break his fall, landed weak and trembling upon the ground beneath. The two Davis boys instantly dropped down to his side; and the three heroes beat a retreat. But, if they could not carry the enemy by boarding, they still had an advantage at long bowls. They stood off and began a shower of rocks from three points at the victim in the tree. But it was a hard target to hit. She was never still, twisting out of sight around the trunk, climbing up and down from branch to branch. And, though one or two rocks struck her glancing blows, she was practically unharmed. However, she had no desire to remain a target. They were crowding in, getting the range, and throwing straighter and faster. Sooner or later she might by knocked from the branches, and then would follow a ducking at the creek that she could never forget.

Presently she slipped out to the end of a branch and concentrated her fire upon Joe Davis, immediately before her. Speed was not what she wanted, but accuracy. She nailed him in the leg with one rock and rapped his ribs with another, and, when he turned about with a yell of pain and anger, she planted a third fairly in the small of his back. It was too much for Joe. When a fourth rock missed his ear by an inch, he fled to the side and out of danger. And that was all the opening that Mary Valentine asked for. She dropped down through the tree—a brown streak—hardly seeming to touch the branches, as she flew past. She hit the ground, running, and darted out through the gap that the desertion of Joe had made. There was a spirited pursuit, but in five minutes she was safe. Not one of the three could match his speed of foot against the flashing lightness of her legs.

She dropped them behind her in a copse and doubled straight back to the village. She was not even panting when she reached the street again, but her eye was like the eye of a hawk. She had not yet extracted from humanity sufficient payment for that blow her uncle had given her. So she went like a poacher among the back yards. And what should she find in the yard of the blacksmith, but an imitation tea in progress—a great bowl of lemonade, standing in the shade of a tree near the carriage shed, and a dozen little girls surrounding it, all in dainty little frocks, with dainty little faces, and sweet, chirping little voices.

The nose of Mary Valentine wrinkled with disdain. If there was a pang in her inmost spirit, it was quickly banished from consciousness. One sharp glance showed her the point of strategic weakness. In an instant, she was up the rear of the shed with a chunk of wood tucked under her arm. Like an Indian, she stole to the front of the little building and leaned out. The shadow of the chunk of wood fell upon the bowl of lemonade beneath. Too late the destined victims looked up and shrieked at the sight of the marauder. For the chunk fell. The lemonade was splashed stickily over a dozen best dresses, and the marauder fled with a whoop of joyous content.

Now there would be twelve complaints lodged by irate fathers with Uncle Marsh before the day was over, and that meant a whipping at dark and supper time, but, for that matter, she would receive one because of the glass she had thrown at her uncle's head, and why not be thrashed for two offenses as well as one? She shrugged her shoulders, and went looking for more adventure. She crossed from the village. She climbed the hill to the west. She looked down to the creek, winding along and lazy through the hollow, with a dense forest crowded on its banks. She looked beyond to the red cattle on the brown hills, to the blue of the horizon sky, to the white sheen of the clouds, which the wind was blowing raggedly above her head. No breath of that wind touched the face of the earth, but, though the sun pressed hot and heavy down upon her, Mary Valentine did not care. Her soul was at rest, since she had extracted from society at large as much pain as she had suffered. And since she had her fill of adventure, she told herself that the next wise step would be to find a shady place by the creek, there to rest, and there, perhaps, to strip off her clothes and slide into the black, silent waters of some pool.

She found the right place. Indeed, there was not an inch

along the winding waters of the creek, within five miles of the village, that she did not know by heart, and she longed, above all things, to wander down its course some day to the great river into which it disappeared. She found the right place near a strip of fresh grass. The sifted sunlight fell upon her through the thin leaves of a willow, so that she could see the blue-white heart of the sky, when the wind stirred the head of the tree. The breeze rose, grew steady, pushed back a large branch, and she was lost in the contemplation of a buzzard, hanging in the keen distance. Suddenly, she heard a noise beside her. It was a faint rustling, and, then, she heard the weight of a footfall pressing the earth. Perhaps Chet and the Davis boys had trailed her, after all. She leaped to her feet and confronted a stranger, an armed man, who at that instant stepped into the little clearing.

There was something about this stranger, armed though he was, that reassured her as to his character.

Mary drew a breath of relief, but the instant her shadow rose, the newcomer had whirled upon her, and in whirling, as though automatically, he brought out the shining length of a Colt revolver and pointed it in her direction. It sent a little shock through Mary. When the muzzle of the gun passed across the line of her body, it was as though a knife had whipped across her. The stranger was trying to smile, as he put up the gun again, but the shadow of seriousness was still behind his eyes, and something told Mary—perhaps it was a sudden pallor that was showing in his cheeks—that he had come within a hairbreadth of planting a bullet in her heart, before he distinguished her as a child—and as a girl.

Chapter Three

" 'Is Your Name Kinkaid?' "

"Well," said Mary, with her usual nonchalance, "the gent that says I'm not born lucky lies."

The stranger was drumming on the handle of his gun as he examined her, and it seemed to Mary that he started a little as she spoke.

"Why lucky?" he asked her.

"How close," said Mary, "did you come to drilling me just then?"

He flushed. "No danger of that," he said, but the flush meant more than the words.

"Maybe not," she said, "if you shoot like most left-handed men that I know of."

He laughed, and, when he laughed, he threw back his head and let the merriment flow freely out from his throat. She liked that about him very much. Uncle Marsh, for instance, never took his eyes from another's face when he laughed.

"What are you doing here?" he asked her.

"Resting," said Mary.

"From what?"

She looked at him closely. He was very, very brown. He was browner, indeed, than she was, and that very brown skin made the blue of his eyes wonderfully intense. He had a thin face, very much drawn of cheek and marked about the eyes, so that Mary thought she had never seen so weary a face. He looked as though he had not slept for a fortnight, and yet there was no seeking for rest in his eyes. She could see at a glance that he was brave. In fact, she was a judge of courage, for she had spent her life surrounded by it, and, though this was hardly the type of fearlessness that showed in the faces of her uncle and her cousins, yet she felt its presence most distinctly. He seemed small, too, compared with those burly giants, yet, when she estimated him with an accurate glance, she knew that he was close to six feet in height; and, though his lower body was wiry and lean, there was promise of great strength in the width of his shoulders.

"I guess I got tired doing the same thing that you been doing," said Mary.

He started again.

"What do you mean by that?" he asked.

"Running away," said Mary.

He could not help flashing a glance over his shoulder; then he centered his stare upon her.

"You're a queer kid," he said. "Suppose we sit down and talk it over."

"Sure," said Mary, and they slumped down upon the turf, side by side.

"What do you mean by me running away?" he asked, rolling his cigarette.

"You might offer me the makings," said Mary.

Once more he seemed surprised. But, at length, he passed the package of brown papers and the sack of tobacco to her.

101

And she made her cigarette with swift exactness, sifting in the correct amount of tobacco with a single flick of the bag and rolling the paper with one twist of the fingers. She lighted the sulphur match with equal skill by whipping the nail of her thumb across its head. Then she shot a thin stream of smoke at the branches above her and leaned back against the trunk of the willow tree, with a sigh of content.

"How long have you been smoking?"

"I dunno that I just exactly remember," said Mary.

"And what have you been running away from?"

"Uncle Marsh."

"What's he done to you?"

"He'll whale me tonight."

"Why?"

"I've been raising ructions."

"Ah," said the stranger, "you have?"

"Ah," mocked Mary, "I have. You talk like a preacher, stranger. What are *you* running away from?"

"I haven't said that I'm running away."

"I can tell, though."

"How?"

"You look twice at everything. Once to see that it's there, and once to see that it ain't sneaking up on you. 'Most like you've plugged somebody."

The stranger smiled.

"You have me stopped," he declared, shifting his holster so that he could sit more comfortably. "Smoking and raising ructions at your age, what'll you be when you grow up?"

"Into a woman?" asked Mary.

"Yep."

"I sure hate to think of that bad time coming."

He laughed again in the hearty way that she liked so much.

"You don't want to grow up, then?"

"Do I look as if I did?"

"You seem contented. When you look over the town, I

suppose that there isn't a single grown girl that you'd care to be like.''

"Only one,'' said Mary, "and it ain't any use to want to be like her.''

"How come?'' said the stranger.

"You're fuller of questions,'' said Mary, "than a prickly pear is full of stickers, Lefty.''

"I carried over being curious out of time when I was a kid. Bad habit I can't get rid of. But why can't you be like the girl you admire?''

Mary sighed. "Look yonder,'' she said, pointing up to the sky beyond the branches. "Can you tell how that there blue is mixed up with sunshine and things so's you can look a million miles into it?''

"No, I can't.''

"She's as different from me,'' said Mary, "as that blue up yonder is different from the blue of these here overalls. Both are kind of faded looking, but they ain't the same.''

He chuckled again. "I suppose she's pretty?''

"Nothing to tell the church about, she ain't. She's got red hair and a stub nose.''

"Ah,'' said Lefty, "red hair?''

"She's got a big mouth, too. And her ears look like they was pinned on her head mighty quick and careless.''

"As bad as all that?''

"Yep . . . worse!''

"What do you like about her?''

"Old son,'' said Mary, "she's got a voice that's the pure quill! I could sit here the rest of my life, if she'd just stay and read to me. She's the teacher over to the school. You see?''

"God bless me,'' said Lefty.

"D'you know her?''

"I'd like to, if she's as fine as that.''

"I ain't got the words for her,'' she assured him.

"What's her name?''

103

"Nancy Pembroke."

"It's a good name," said Lefty. "I'll bet she'd be a pal."

"She wouldn't," said Mary. "She's got no use for men."

"How come?"

"She was about to tie up to a gent some three or four years back, but he busted loose and bumped off a man just before the ceremony. He had to run for it, and ever since that time she's been thinking about nobody but him."

Lefty leaned forward upon his hands and stared at Mary, as though she were a ghost.

"D'you mean that?" he asked.

"What's up?"

"Nothing."

"You look sort of sick. Did you know Kinkaid?"

"Does she tell that name around?"

"She says that she ain't ashamed. She says that she cares more for him than ever."

"Oh, Lord," groaned Lefty, "what a woman she is." And he let his eyes wander past Mary and far among the trees.

"Lefty," said Mary presently.

"Well?" he murmured.

"I'd like to ask you a question. Will you answer it?"

"If it ain't too long."

"One word'll answer it, Lefty."

"Fire away, then."

"Is your name Kinkaid?"

Chapter Four

"Markle"

Having watched and talked all night and all the evening before and all the morning that followed, Marsh Valentine and his sons went to bed at noon and slept until five. When they wakened, as of one accord, they yawned the sleep out of their throats and stretched it out of their iron muscles, and so they were ready for action of any kind again. Their tremendous bodies were unimpaired by the long watch and the short sleep, but their tempers were wolfish. They cooked and ate an evening breakfast without speaking to one another. As they sat about on the verandah of the shack, smoking their cigarettes and scowling at the wind that blew hot in their faces, Mary Valentine came home. The manner of her coming was as strange as the manner of her leaving that morning.

She appeared out of the heart of the dusk and came straight up to Uncle Marsh. She stood before him with her arms folded across her breast and her feet braced, as though against the expected shock of a heavy blow.

"Well," she said, "here I am. I'm ready to take what's coming to me."

Uncle Marsh regarded her in silence. His hand twitched, and his frown grew murderously black. He even settled a little forward in his chair, and his two sons watched anxiously. If the big man put forth even a fraction of his strength, it was certain that he would crush the frail body of the child and the life hidden within it. But finally, with a shrug of his heavy shoulders, he settled back in his chair. "Get inside," he said. Mary glided softly through the door.

"What you going to do to her?" asked Oliver.

"You couldn't guess in a thousand years."

"Couldn't?"

"No . . . I'm going to do nothing to her."

"What?"

"Lemme tell you something, Oliver, the gent that lays hands on that little devil will get his throat cut for his trouble."

"You're afraid of her, then," grinned Oliver.

"Ain't you?"

"I dunno but I am," said Oliver. "But I thought that you was going to bust her in two when she stood up to you."

"I was ashamed for what I done this morning," said Uncle Marsh slowly. "I didn't think . . . I just hit. And it sort of did me good when she got up and threw that glass at me. If I'd caught her, I'd have told her I was sorry that I'd hit her. Believe me, I'd rather take a beating than do what I did then."

Glances were exchanged sharply between the two sons. There was no doubt at all that they were glad to hear this conclusion.

"Going to tell her that now?"

"Nope. She's been a rebel, and she's got to pay for it. There's only one way to rule a Valentine, and that's with fear. She'll be afraid now for days and days that she's about to get paid for what she done today, and that'll keep her in hand. Otherwise, there wouldn't be no living with her."

"Did you ever try kindness?" asked Jack Valentine.

"I ain't a fool. When she first come to me, I took one look at them eyes of hers, and I knew what she needed was a whip. She's a Valentine, and the Valentines make a pile better men than women. But if. . . ." Here he broke off short, for Oliver had raised his hand for silence.

"What is it?" asked the father.

"I heard a whistle."

"Keep quiet, then. If it's the whistle I expect, it'll come again."

And come again it did, with a peculiar falling note at the end, like the whistle of a bird.

"It's Markle," said the father.

It brought the two sons out of their chairs.

"Sit down," he commanded. "Are you going to act like Markle was the devil just come up from hell?"

"Ain't that what he is?"

"Pretty close to that, but I'd rather be turned to a cinder than have him know that I think him anything."

"Dad, you're kind of afraid of him, yourself!"

"A gent that ain't afraid of Markle is a fool. Are you afraid of poison? Are you afraid of a snake?"

"Then why work with him?"

"We ain't working with him, yet. Ain't much chance that we will. But we're just going to listen to him talk. Understand?"

There were nods from the sons. And presently straight up the slope in front of the house jogged a horseman. Even in the saddle he seemed extraordinarily short. He looked more like a mounted sack than a mounted man. He slid down to the ground and advanced. And, as he walked, his size was shown in a more ludicrous light, for he was not a breath over five feet in height, and yet the horse which he bestrode was a monster, even larger than those huge animals that were now munching hay in the Valentine barn, animals capable of supporting all the Valentine bulk. This magnificent beast was perhaps a shade under seventeen hands and gloriously muscled. He was as huge and as statuesque among horses as his rider was blunt and misshapen among men.

He came squarely into the range of the light that shone through the open doorway from the interior of the house, where Mary was foraging for supplies in the kitchen, sending out a faint chiming of pans now and again. It seemed very strange that this outlawed man should have come up so boldly, without waiting to reconnoiter, and should now stand where the light fell upon a head worth thousands and thousands of dollars to the man whose lucky bullet should bring him down to the earth.

Grotesque he certainly was. His head was a pyramid, of which a wide, bulging jaw was the base, and the narrowing forehead was the blunt apex. His nose was as flat as that of a pugilist who had been hammered to a pulp a hundred times. His little eyes peered out from beneath great flabby lids which seemed to be raised only with a pronounced effort. His head was placed upon his shoulders without the support of a neck, and his body was a rounded barrel. His legs were two diminutive pipe stems, utterly inadequate to support such a burden, and, therefore, they sagged in sadly at the knees.

For a moment he remained in the shaft of light, as though he wished each of the three shadowy giants to see his face distinctly. Then he advanced to Marsh, who had risen to meet him. They shook hands in silence, and then the sons were presented; to them Markle spoke freely enough.

"I've been waiting to see you for three years," he said. "I've tried a dozen times to get in touch with you, but you been moving so fast that I ain't ever come up with you. But now that I'm here, I'll say that I'm mighty glad to see you both. It ain't the last that we're going to meet."

"Maybe not," said Marsh Valentine, "but the boys don't take to the job that you got in mind. I ain't been able to tell them no particulars, but they don't cotton to the idea."

"They're figuring on going straight, I guess," said Markle, looking from one young giant to the other.

"That's it."

"Do they think they can do it?"

"They do."

"All young men are blockheads," said Markle, and he took a chair and tilted it back against the wall.

There was no answer. None of them would have taken so much from any other human being, but Markle was different. To challenge him meant to challenge his gun, and to challenge his gun was to flirt with death. Besides, he was rolling a cigarette, and his manner was far more amiable than his words. The other three sat down.

"I dunno," said Marsh. "I can't say that I'm trying to persuade 'em any, Markle."

"How d'you figure on going straight?"

"Starting in cowpunching," said Oliver.

"Have you hunted for a job yet?"

"Only asked a couple."

"Had any luck?"

"Both outfits was full up."

Markle snorted. "There ain't a big outfit in the mountains that's too full up to need a Valentine," he said. "There ain't an outfit in the range that don't know that any Valentine can do two men's work. Why, Oliver, ain't it said that you never been throwed from a hoss, and that you can break six bad 'uns a day and keep it up for a month?"

"I dunno that I'm as good as all that," said Oliver, "but I have a way with hosses."

"You're as good as that, and better. I've heard about your work. And there's Jack, that's sure death with a rope. Jack knows the points of a cowpuncher's work like it was all wrote down in a book that he knowed by heart. No, partners, there ain't a bunch on the range that wouldn't be glad to have you."

"But they're full-handed, the two we asked."

"They lied. Everybody's short-handed this season. Everybody's looking for more men."

"Why should they turn us down, then?"

"Because they don't trust you."

"The governor gave us a pardon."

"The governor pardoned you, but the gents around these parts ain't the governor."

"What do you mean by that?"

"They all think that you're crooked. I've heard 'em talk. They think that every Valentine is a crook. And they'll never hire you."

There was a growl from the two.

"We'll prove that we're straight, though," said Jack.

"How much money have you got laid by?" asked Markle of the father.

There was no answer for a moment.

"I've been in bad luck. I ain't got any money laid by."

"Son," said the outlaw, "you'll starve before you get through proving your point. You'll starve, I say, and, when you got to have food to put inside of you, you'll have to go and take it. That's the way, always. They think you done the thing you were blamed for. They hunted you for three years, and they'll keep on hunting you, no matter what the governor says. You ain't got a chance!"

Silence came heavily upon the group for a time.

"Is that right, Dad?" asked Oliver.

"I dunno," said Marsh miserably. "I dunno what to say to you."

"Ask yourselves," said Markle.

"We have been asking ourselves."

"And even if you got a job, would you be able to hold it down? For three years you been free. Can you settle down and take the orders of a foreman that you could bust in two between your hands?''

''It'd be hard,'' admitted Oliver.

''It ain't possible, son. I'm talking because I want you with me, but I'm telling you the truth at the same time.''

''We can test things out.''

''If you wait for that time, I won't be here. I've come to offer you a fine chance, Oliver and Jack.''

''Tell us the game.''

''There's a hundred thousand of the long green in the bank right this here minute.''

''Bank robbery!'' exclaimed Jack.

''Wait a minute,'' said Oliver. ''Might as well be something big as something little. What's the plan?''

''A mighty easy one. I got six men with me. They're all hardboiled. They're all hard riders and straight shooters, and they all would stick close together. There ain't a one of the six that ain't killed his man. There ain't a one of the six that wouldn't hang if he was captured. So they'll all fight till they drop. That's the kind of men that I like to have around me. Those six and you two and me make nine men. I'd come straight into town tomorrow afternoon about the middle of the. . . .''

''And let people see you?''

''They'd never recognize me. They might know my picture, but they won't believe their eyes when they see me riding into town. And they'll go right on about their business and leave me to mine. Then I put five men around the bank to watch the horses and keep away the crowd, when folks starts to coming. With the other four we go into the bank, and I walk up to the cashier's window and shove a gun under his nose. The other three keep the boys in the bank covered, and I make them dish out the stuff that's in the safe. Ain't that simple?''

''Simple,'' said Oliver, ''but it means a killing.''

''Of who . . . the cashier?''

111

"I know the cashier."

"So do I, and I got him fixed. He's working with me. You'd say that cashier would get himself killed rather than give up, but I knowed that, and I fixed him right. He'll do what me and the gun tell him to do."

"Are you sure?"

"Absolute."

"But what if old man Preston is around?"

"He's a fighter, but he's ready for a funeral, anyway. He's done his killings in his day, and it's turn and turn about. He's got to take his medicine if he asks for it tomorrow."

Oliver shook his head. "It won't do," he said. "I can't do the work. I go straight, or I go bust. That's all there is to it."

"Wait!" said Markle suddenly, raising his hand. After a moment he added: "Somebody's coming. I'll just go inside." And he walked indifferently into the house.

Chapter Five

"The Pact"

He had disappeared through the door and settled himself quietly before they heard the noise that the keen ear of the outlaw had detected. Then they made out the steady and muffled beating of the hoofs of a horse in the dust which led up from the village street.

"How could he have heard it?" asked Oliver, touched with awe by the acute senses of the outlaw.

"Living wild and free for half the years of his life is what made him sharp at hearing," said the father. "They say that Markle can hear a whisper clear across a room while he's sound asleep."

"They say that he can shoot a knothole out of a board at fifty yards, while his hoss is galloping, too," said Oliver scornfully.

"He can," said the father, "because I seen him do it!"

This amazing announcement caused a gasp of interest, but

there was no further opportunity for talk. The horseman took shape in the night, halted his animal, and dismounted just before them. He called before he approached.

"Are you there, Marsh?"

"Here!" answered Valentine, and he added in a swift whisper to his sons: "It's Sheriff Aldridge!"

The two big men stiffened in their places. For three years the famous sheriff had trailed them, and, indeed, he had been about to bag them when the pardon of the governor cut the knot which he had tied about them. Now the sheriff approached and stood near the verandah.

"Sit down," invited Marsh Valentine.

The sheriff dismissed the invitation with a wave of his hand.

"I'll stand," he asserted. "I been sitting in the saddle till my legs are sort of cramped. Marsh, is this Oliver, and is that Jack?"

"Right."

"I'm glad I found you all three together. I got something to say that you'll all have to hear sooner or later."

"Come right out with it, Aldridge."

"Marsh, I got to talk pretty straight to you."

"Fire away. Everybody knows that you ain't got any store of soft words, Sheriff."

The sternness of the sheriff was known and dreaded for a thousand miles among the mountains. He was as keen as a ferret upon the trail and almost as relentless.

"I come up here to say that Markle ain't far away!"

It was a stunning blow. None of the three could speak for an instant, and each one of them covertly strained his eyes toward the trees that encircled the house at a little distance. For, if the sheriff had guessed at the coming of Markle, he would certainly not attempt to make that capture without assistance. The woods must be full of the men he had brought to assist in the great work. For, though it was ordinarily to be expected that one sheriff was equal to one criminal, it was foolhardy to presume that any one man was the match of Markle.

The sheriff went on speaking: "Maybe you've seen him."

"I ain't flush," said Marsh Valentine, answering indirectly. "I guess that I could use the money on Markle's head as good as the next man!"

"Well," said the sheriff, "I'm not a mind reader. All I can say is that Markle has sneaked into the mountains near here, and that we're watching for him. He's got no friends in this here town. I can swear to that, and the game ain't running very thick in the mountains. That means he'll be drawing on somebody for supplies if he can, and I sure hope that he ain't drawing on you, Valentine."

Marsh Valentine shrugged his wide shoulders. "I ain't a fool, Sheriff. I've had trouble enough with the law without wanting to get burned again."

"If I could be sure of that . . . but I can't be sure of anything, Marsh. I ain't saying that you lie. All I say is that you and me have never had a real brush, and I'm hoping that we never do have one. But, if I find out anybody that's having dealings with Markle, it'll go hard with him. And them that deal with him is the same as him. I'll treat 'em that way!"

Here Jack Valentine could bear it no longer. "Are you aiming that talk at me and Oliver?" he asked.

"I'm aiming it at nobody, Jack," said the sheriff. "But I sure want you and Oliver to watch yourselves half as close as I'm watching you. You had luck with me once, but you ain't going to have no luck the second time."

"You've talked enough for me to know your drift," said Oliver. "You can move on, Sheriff. I'll ride clean into your office and give you a call when I want your helping words. Understand?"

"Trouble breeds trouble," said the sheriff darkly. "I been waiting for it to crop up out here in this house for a good long time, and I guess it's about due to arrive. If there's a sign of Markle having got a grubstake from you, I'll come out here raising more trouble than you ever dreamed of seeing. So long!''

And swinging with graceful ease back into the saddle, he made off through the night once more. The quiet was thick and heavy that he left behind him, and into it stepped the pudgy figure of Markle. He was laughing softly, and at every wave of his laughter the two big men winced.

''Well, boys,'' he said, ''there's the start of the square deal that you're waiting for. How'd you like it?''

Jack Valentine sprang to his feet.

''I'm with you, Markle!'' he cried. ''I've sat here and listened to myself being insulted. If they already think that we're men of your gang, why shouldn't we go ahead and be what they think? But when we get into your harness, we're going to move such a load that they'll wish we was the other side of the sun. Oliver, are you with me?''

''Wait a minute before you answer!'' broke in Marsh. ''Boys, you got to take this here thing sober. What you decide now is going to make the rest of your lives.''

''I'm ready to decide,'' answered Oliver. ''I want to wring the neck of Aldridge. After that I don't much care what happens to us.''

''Leave Aldridge out of it,'' said Marsh Valentine. ''He ain't as bad as you think. Never framed a gent in his life. I'll say that for Aldridge. Besides, it was sort of honest for him to come right up here and give us a warning.''

''Honest? What he wanted was a chance to insult us, knowing that we wouldn't tackle the sheriff unless we had to.''

''Maybe not, boys. Aldridge ain't any smooth talker, but there ain't nobody ever accused him of lying.''

''I accuse him now. Markle, I'm with you!''

And Markle shook that great hand and the hand of the other brother, while Marsh sank back in his chair with a groan, as he saw that the compact was made.

"What's the matter?" said Markle. "I didn't ask you to let me at 'em!"

"I thought they'd stand up ag'in' the gaff," muttered Marsh Valentine. "But they buckled up. They couldn't hold out ag'in' temptation."

"Well," said Markle, "it's only them that are in it. You'll be safe enough out of the game tomorrow."

"Me out? You couldn't keep me out! Me out with my two lads in?"

"You'll come in, Marsh?"

"To the limit!"

"Will you shake on the deal?"

"I will, but no thanks to you." Their hands closed. "You've sold the whole family," said Marsh Valentine. "And now get out, Markle, before we change our minds!"

Markle waited for no second invitation. He waved his hand to them and strolled off into the dark. Then they heard him talking to himself, as he dragged himself into the saddle. "We'll come by this way and pick you up tomorrow," he called. "By the way, old Aldridge is kind of partial to me, eh?"

And he was still laughing at his jest, as he rode away into the night.

"Dad," said Oliver.

"Well?" asked the old man, lifting his head slowly from the hand upon which he had dropped it.

"I got an idea that Markle was doing all that talking to us just to pull you into his gang."

"D'you figure that out, too? Then you're wiser than I took you to be, Oliver! Yep, that's what the hound wants. And he's got it!"

"But we," cried Jack, "will get in our crack at Aldridge."

"And the hundred thousand!" said Oliver.

Chapter Six

"On Business Bent"

On the steep roof above the verandah Mary Valentine uncurled herself from the cramped position in which she had been lying. She had overheard everything that passed beneath her, and she had understood. That is, she has heard everything since the arrival of the sheriff, and her mind was humming with the new information. What Markle was she knew partly by rumor, which had touched her attention, and still more by the sound of his voice and the words he had spoken. And she realized that here was one who was as formidable as either her uncle or her two great cousins.

She went slowly, slowly up the incline of the roof. It had been comparatively simple to make the descent without a noise, but it was painfully hard to make the ascent. Indeed, just before she reached the window, a shingle creaked beneath her weight. There was an exclamation from the verandah beneath her and then a rush up the stairs.

Through the window went Mary with the agility of a cat.
And into her room she raced and flung herself on the bed.
Footfalls rushed swiftly past her door and, then, to the window overlooking the verandah roof.

"Nothing here?"

"Look in Mary's room. Maybe it was her."

At the door, presently, loomed the great form of Oliver.
He strode into the room, none too lightly, scratched a match,
and, as the flame spurted blue from the sulphur head, he
looked down and surveyed her.

She could only pray that her eyelids would not quiver,
or that the heaving of her bosom would not betray that she
was panting for breath. Indeed, in the struggle to control
that breathing, she was almost stifled. But, presently, the
big hand of Oliver gripped her shoulder and raised her to a
sitting posture. She blinked her eyes at him rapidly and
yawned.

"What's up?" asked Mary. "Got the makings, Ollie?"

"Forget the makings," grunted Oliver. "What I want to
know is how long you been asleep here?"

"I dunno," said Mary. "I was plumb beat. I went to sleep
without undressing. Is it midnight, Ollie?"

"It ain't," said Oliver, and he let her fall back upon the
bed.

Then he left the room, and, as he went back to the verandah, Mary slipped to the front upstairs window again. She
could hear them talking, at first very softly and then with
more confidence, as they heard the report of Oliver.

"She was asleep," said Oliver.

"How did you know?" asked his father. "She could play
dead like a rabbit, the little fox!"

"She had all the look of it in her eyes," said Oliver.
"She'd been sound asleep, all right. She wanted to know if
it was midnight." And he chuckled.

"If you start in believing what she says," declared Uncle

Marsh, "she'll give you enough inside of a day for a whole book. There's some that got to study lying. But Mary was just born with a lot of talent for saying things that ain't true. She can make up lies faster'n Markle can fan a gun."

"Does Markle fan a gun?"

"He does."

"I've heard talk about fanning, but I ain't ever seen it done."

"Markle does it."

"But can he hit anything when he fans his gun?"

"I've seen him knock over a rabbit."

There was a groan of astonishment from the two boys, and Mary went back to her room. There she took the parcel of food that she had prepared in the kitchen. There was a loaf of bread and a liberal chunk of ham, a pound of coffee, and a small portion of salt. She wrapped the package in an outer layer of paper and, then, made her exit through the window. A drainage pipe ran down from the eaves near her window, and she held the package with her teeth and lowered herself, hand over hand, to the ground with the easy agility of a monkey.

As she went toward the village, she bumped her toe on a stump and recalled that one calamity had been spared her that day—this was the news of her exploit with the bowl of lemonade and the splashed dresses. That escapade had not been revealed to Uncle Marsh. Otherwise, there would have been a whipping. But, perhaps, this punishment as well as that for her revolt of the morning was being saved against a time when Uncle Marsh should have conceived a torment great enough to balance against her misdeeds.

However, before that time of punishment came, Uncle Marsh and both of her cousins would be far away from her. They would be hounded across the country as bank robbers. Mary stopped short and shook her head, as that awful thought came home to her again. Markle, she knew, was charged with a score of murders which were known and proved, and there were others that were guessed at. Perhaps Uncle Marsh and his sons would soon be in the same category with the famous outlaw.

At this, she rubbed the shin of her left leg with the toes of her right, standing balanced, with the surety of a crane, upon one foot. No doubt such a calamity would free her from the strict government of Uncle Marsh, but it was also to be considered that Uncle Marsh was not altogether to be despised or hated. That he was strict had to be admitted, but he could also be kind. Ordinarily he paid not the slightest attention to her, but on that grim day, when her father died, she could not forget how the giant had come to her and taken her tenderly in his arms and promised her a home. And she could not forget, also, that, when she had been sick on two occasions, Uncle Marsh would allow no one to nurse her but himself, that he had remained day and night beside her bed, and that the strength of his great hands had seemed to bring her back to life. It was no wonder, therefore, that her opinion of Uncle Marsh was a mixed one. And if on the one hand she dreaded him like death, on the other hand she respected him with a mighty reverence.

But, above all, she had a pride in her clan, a pride that was like a fire burning in her breast. She had walked the village street straighter and prouder because her uncle was the strongest old man in the mountains, and her two cousins the strongest of the younger men. She rejoiced in the awe with which others looked upon the three.

But to be known as members of a gang of robbers—to serve under the leadership of a murderer, a stone-hearted killer who had taken lives for hire—this was too much. And solemnly she revolved the problem of how she should stave off the calamity. For, after it happened, she could never again lift her head. She would be shamed for the rest of her days.

When she started on her way, it was at a swift jog, so

great was her haste, and so sudden the inspiration that had startled her. She headed straight into the village and did not slacken her gait until she had arrived at a deserted shack on the outskirts of the town, upon the farther side. Its age was presumably not very great, but paint had never shielded its boards from the cruel weather, and rains and winds and warping suns had wrenched it askew and made all of its cracks gape. It staggered to one side away from the northern winds that came combing down the valley, and the ruins of a shed nearby seemed to prophesy the collapse of the house itself. It was the handwriting upon the wall.

Yet it was at this house that Mary Valentine stopped and rapped faintly at the door. And the door, after a chair had been pushed noisily back, was opened by the sheriff. For this was his home. He tamped down the burning tobacco in his pipe with a callused forefinger, and Mary wondered the hot coal did not singe him to the very flesh. But he removed his finger tip, snapped the ashes from it, wiped it upon his hip, and finally spoke.

"Well, Mary," he said, "what in tarnation have you been up to now?"

She was by no means unhappy to postpone the statement of her real errand, and she welcomed this oblique opening.

"How come," said Mary, "that you figure that I been doing something wrong, Sheriff?"

The sheriff sighed. "When folks do little things," he said, "they let other people tell about it. But when they're pretty deep stuck in the mud, they snoop around to see what the law is going to do to them."

"Well," said Mary, "maybe you're wrong."

"Well," said the sheriff, "maybe I ain't. By the way, Mister and Missus Thomas came up and called on me to-day."

"Has that got something to do with me?" asked Mary, cocking her head anxiously to one side.

"Nothing much. They figure you ought to be sent some

place where you can be looked after, if your uncle can't handle it. And I guess that Marsh Valentine would admit that you're more than a handful.''

"I dunno what you mean," said Mary, "unless it's because that freckle-faced Thomas girl got splashed with a little lemonade today. Is that it?''

"Why did you do it?'' asked the sheriff curiously. ''Those girls weren't bothering you, Mary.,''

"They looked plumb silly," said Mary, "standing around and trying to talk like growed-ups. It made me so tired I ached. I had to bust up the party, so I took the shortest way to the finish. Wouldn't you have wanted to do the same thing?''

"Maybe," said the sheriff, but he remained very grave.

She studied him as fixedly as he studied her.

"I know what you think," said Mary. "You figure that all the Valentines are bad, and that I'm as bad as the rest. Is that it?''

"Of course not!''

"You're sort of polite, but I know what's behind your eyes. Well, Mister Sheriff, you're all wrong. Look here, the Valentines were as good as any people in the world. Then along came Uncle Marsh and his two sons, and they're so dog-gone big that everybody expects them to bust heads. And because everybody stands around plumb *expecting* trouble from Uncle Marsh and Ollie and Jack, they get trouble . . . and a whole fistful of it, too! Ain't that reasonable?''

"Mary," said the sheriff, "where did you hear that?''

"Look here," said Mary, "if I act like I was afraid of Sammy Davis in the school yard, Sammy's going to start bothering me and trying to pull my hair and a whole lot of other fool things. But if I act like Sammy Davis was a worm I could squash with a look, he don't bother me none at all. Ain't I right, Sheriff Aldridge?''

The sheriff coughed and then rubbed his knuckles across his chin.

"Come inside and set yourself down, Mary," he said. And he stood back from the door to let her pass.

Chapter Seven

"The Sheriff Laughs"

Only those who lived in that county could appreciate the honor that had been bestowed upon Mary. For the sheriff had no friends near and dear enough to ask into his house. He lived resolutely alone, and he had done so since the landslide carried away his wife and his son, eight years before. That had made him an old man at a stroke, and it had also made him a misanthrope and a hermit. If he was elected sheriff, it was not that people were fond of him, but because he was infinitely respected. They were too much afraid of him to pity him, but he was elected because he was needed.

Among the mountains that surrounded the town there were a thousand nests where outlaws could secret themselves, to issue forth like storms at times of advantage and harry the countryside. Many an industrious rancher had been ruined by the constant rustling of his cows, and many a hard-working miner had been cleaned out of his season's gold by a stick-up artist with a gun. So the district needed a sheriff who was something more than a name and a badge, and Sheriff Aldridge was the man. He had thrown his blanket in this wretched shack. In the ramshackle barn there was room for his three fine horses, whose color was known five hundred miles on every side. And the sheriff was as firmly fixed in his office as a man who is lashed into the saddle.

The room in which Mary found herself lived up to what tradition had said about the sheriff. It was a long and narrow apartment, that was used by him for the three purposes of cooking, eating, and sleeping. The rest of the house was obviously abandoned. But there was a stove in one end of the room, with a bunk against the wall at the other end, and two old saddles, bridles, all manner of riding gear, spurs, guns, boots, belts, hats, hanging in clouds from the pegs that went down either wall.

As for his official correspondence, he had a little lame-legged desk in one corner. This, then, was the habitation of the most efficient sheriff along the entire range. As for what he spent his money on, Mary could not imagine, though rumor said that he simply put it in the bank and there let it lie, accumulating interest simply because he did not know what to do with it. The cost of his horses and their feed, the price of his guns and their ammunition, of which he consumed enough for an hour's practice every day, the price of his provisions, which were of the simplest imaginable— these were the only objects upon which he expended a penny, with the exception of his tobacco. For he had worn the same clothes for a dozen years, and, though they were ingrained of dust and dirt, the sheriff paid no heed. "The slicker they are, the easier they fit in the saddle," he was fond of saying.

He pointed to a chair—it was the only one in the room— and, when Mary sat down in it, he slouched down upon the bunk and rolled a cigarette.

"Got enough for another?" asked Mary.

He hesitated, just so long as a man hesitates before he draws a gun, then, perfectly grave, he passed the makings to her.

"I forgot that you smoke," said the sheriff, and, having waited for her to make her smoke, he lighted them both with the same match.

"Now," he said, "the way I make it out is that the Valentines are good, honest, law-fearing gents. Is that it, Mary?"

"That's it," she answered calmly. "Except that they don't fear nothing, and you know it."

A shadow of a grin appeared at the corners of the sheriff's mouth.

"What's that?" he asked, pointing to the bundle of food that she carried.

"A present," said Mary.

"Ah?" said the sheriff.

"If I show it to you, will you keep the secret of who it's meant for?"

"Why is it a secret?"

"You'd be glad to know," said Mary, who now had the conversation back on the track on which she wished it.

"Fire away, then."

"I'll have to have your promise."

"Is it for Markle?"

She started to answer, then sat back in her chair with a smile.

"Very well," said the sheriff, grinning at the adroitness with which she had avoided his remark. "But I give no promises, till I know what they're about."

Mary bowed her head in thought. She had not expected that the way would be quite as hard as this, but, as she listened, she heard a voice singing in the distance, a voice that pierced small and sharp through the walls of the shaky house, a voice infinitely sweet and tender. And Mary, raising

127

her small head, heard and recognized the singing of Nancy Pembroke.

"D'you know who's singing?" she asked.

"Yes," said the sheriff, "it's Nancy, of course."

Mary blinked at him, but, after all, there was nothing strange in the ease with which he recognized Nancy's voice, for her sweet singing was known to the whole village. Yet, who could have expected the iron sheriff to have opened his mind to such a thing as music?

"Well," said Mary, "this has something to do with Nancy."

"Of course," said the sheriff, "if it has anything to do with her, I'll give you my promise. I won't use nothing that you may tell me."

Mary breathed a great sigh, so keen was her relief.

"I'll put it to you this way," she said. "Suppose that a gent was overdue to go to meet a girl that he loved . . . suppose that, while he was riding, he comes acrost a man he'd had trouble with before . . . suppose the other man tries to start a fight and finally gets what he wants . . . suppose that the first man drops him and kills him in a square fight. Now, suppose that a crooked pal of the dead man seen the fight from a distance and rides into town and tells a lie about how his partner was *murdered*."

"Ah," said the sheriff.

"Well," said Mary, "that's what happened with Lefty Kinkaid."

The sheriff started up from the bunk.

"Is Lefty near here?" he asked with fire in his eye.

"Sure," said Mary. "I'm taking this chuck to him down by the creek."

The sheriff, in place of answering with words, merely scooped up his hat and jammed it upon his head.

"You gave me a promise," said Mary.

"What's Lefty got to do with Nancy Pembroke?"

"He was going to marry her, that's all, and he's come

back to these parts just to see her. I'll bet you that Nancy has come back from seeing him right now. Listen!''

The singing had been drawing steadily closer and closer, and, now, it turned a corner and swelled suddenly beside them. It passed. It turned another corner and was presently fading.

''My sakes,'' said Mary, as she twisted her feet under her and sat cross-legged in the chair, ''ain't Nancy happy?''

The sheriff was chewing his lips savagely, his eyes glancing from one side to the other.

''Very well,'' he said at last, ''you may be right. You may be right . . . and you're a clever little demon, Mary!'' He turned upon her again, jerking his sombrero lower over his eyes. ''What in the name of sin do you want out of me?'' he asked her pointblank.

''Would you listen to me?''

''Yes,'' said the sheriff softly, for his head was still raised to hear the last and dying notes of Nancy's song in the distance. ''But why are you so much interested in Nancy's affairs?''

''She's treated me white,'' said Mary, half choked with emotion. ''She's been square with me.''

''And Lefty?''

''Look here,'' said Mary, ''what'd you rather do than anything in the world?''

''You make that guess for me, Mary.''

''You'd rather catch Markle.''

''What d'you know about him?'' asked the sheriff, changing color.

''Suppose that Lefty was to nail him?'' asked Mary. ''Would Lefty be pardoned?''

''A dozen like Lefty would be pardoned if they got rid of one like Markle!''

''Would you shake on that?''

''Maybe I would.''

''Here's my hand,'' said Mary.

And the sheriff took it, still hesitating, still studying her rather desperately and not able to make out what he wished to understand.

"But you know that one man could never nail Markle?" he told her. "You know that Markle may have a dozen hard ones all around him, and every man able to fight like a tiger?"

"I know that," said Mary. "If Markle was cleaned out and his gang with him, there'd be reputations made, eh?"

"Reputation enough for twenty men!"

Mary uncrossed her legs and stood up, yawning. "I got to be going," she said.

"So long," said the sheriff, "and good luck, Mary."

"Thanks," she answered and sauntered to the door.

"But what if your man don't win out?" asked the sheriff.

"There ain't a chance of him losing," said Mary.

"Why not?"

"Didn't you hear Nancy Pembroke singing?"

"Well," said the sheriff, "even a pretty voice can't do everything in the world."

"There's another reason Lefty can't lose," said Mary.

"Let me hear that one."

"Because I'm going to be there to put the business through."

And she disappeared through the doorway. As for the sheriff, he threw back his head and broke into laughter that stopped very short in the middle. He had listened to his own mirth and realized, with amazement, that he had not laughed like this for eight years.

Chapter Eight

"Two Letters"

"There's only one way that you can get back on your feet as an honest man," said Mary.

Lefty, his mouth too full of the provisions she had brought him to answer at once, stopped chewing and stared at her, as though his eyes would pop out from their sockets. When he had finally swallowed and could speak, he gasped: "What do you mean, Mary?"

"I mean Markle. If you was to get Markle, everything would be squared up. The sheriff would get your pardon from the governor. What's more, everybody would figure that you was a sort of a hero, Lefty."

"If I beat Markle and his gang, I would be," grinned Lefty. "There ain't a chance, Mary. I'd need a dozen men to back me."

"Any Valentine," said Mary, "is as good as three other

131

men. Suppose you have my uncle and his two sons behind you?''

''Count them each for three,'' said Lefty, still grinning. ''That's only nine men. Where are the other three, Mary?''

''I'm a Valentine,'' said Mary, ''and I'd come along.''

So they laughed together.

''Do you mean that I could get your uncle and your two cousins to work with me?'' asked Lefty more seriously.

''Wait a minute,'' said Mary, ''because I'm sure thinking hard.''

She lifted her head. Above her the trees swayed like smoke above the small light of the campfire. Past the trees a star or two looked down at her.

''Lefty,'' she said, ''you'll win, or you'll die. D'you love Nancy enough for that?''

''To win her, or else die trying? I do, partner.''

''She sure loves you, Lefty.''

''I dunno why,'' said Lefty, ''but it really looks as though she does.''

''Well,'' said Mary, ''dog-goned if it don't look as though I got to find a way to pull you right out of the fire.''

So she stood up and began to pace rapidly back and forth, smoking at a great rate and scowling at the shaken flame of the fire and the unearthly bodies of the trees, half buried in the night around her. Then, under the weight of an inspiration, she paused. The idea grew large; she clasped her hands together.

''Lefty,'' she cried, ''have you got a hoss?''

''I have.''

''Will you loan him to me?''

''Partner,'' said Lefty, ''ask me for my right arm and my right hand, and throw in my left, too . . . but don't ask me for my hoss. Can't you use one of your uncle's?''

''He ain't got any hosses,'' said Mary. ''He's got a bunch of mountains. They're strong enough to hold up the sky, but they ain't fast enough to catch up with a fat pig. I need some speed tonight.''

"How do you know that my hoss is fast?'' asked Lefty curiously. "You've never seen her.''

"If she wasn't fast, you'd have been stretching a rope a long time back,'' said Mary. "Make up your mind quick, Lefty. Are you going to take a long chance and lemme have the hoss, or are you going to admit you're beat before the game begins?''

"How am I beat so long as Nancy stays by me?''

"What good can you do for her unless you got a pardon? Will you tell me that? All you can do is to spoil her life by keeping her from marrying somebody else.''

Lefty sighed, as the truth of this remark pressed grimly home in him. "What's your plan, Mary?''

"I ain't talking till I can show some results.''

"Not a word?''

"Not a word!''

Without further comment, he rose, disappeared among the trees, and in five minutes returned with a gray mare, like a lovely ghost of a horse in the pale light. She tossed her head, looked this way and that, and finally walked up to the fire and sniffed at it, crouching like a great cat, ready to spring away to safety.

"I got her when she was a little filly hardly up to your hip,'' said Lefty gently. "I raised her by hand till I got her to what you see her now. It ain't easy to hand her over, Mary.''

"I'll treat her like she was mine,'' she assured him. "Will you shorten up the stirrups?''

And, advancing confidently toward the mare, Lefty hesitatingly went forward to do as she bade, still doubtful. The careless assurance of Mary's approach seemed to carry him before her. And Mary scrambled into the saddle and shortened the stirrup upon one side, while Lefty shortened the other, and then she gathered the reins.

"Start straight on for the Valentine house," she advised him. "And when you get there, wait. No, you can do better than that. You can go straight into the house and start making friends with Uncle Marsh. You show him that you need him, and tell him what for and why. Before you get through talking, I'll be back. If he's got any doubt about tying up with you, he'll get over it before I'm through with my game. So long, Lefty."

"Wait!" cried Lefty. "I don't know that I'm going through with this deal. I dunno what. . . ."

Lefty reached for the bridle of the gray, but she was away as smoothly as running water and as suddenly as a bullet from a gun. And though Lefty shouted once after her, she was already out of sight under the trees and the dark, and he could only hear the noise of the mare, as she tore through the wood.

Her plan, so quickly born, had seemed to the girl a foolish thing at first, but, when she sat in the saddle upon the mare and felt all of that strength and that speed poured forth according to her touch upon the reins, she began to think that there must be some power in her worth considering. And the plan, that had appeared such an airy phantasm, now was a solid possibility. On the back of the gray mare one could not ride forth to a failure.

She went straight as an arrow back to the Valentine house. She entered with the softness of a shadow when she had tethered the mare in the woods. On the way up to her room she looked in upon the conclave of the three. The adventures of the years could not be all told in a single sitting, no matter how prolonged, and, therefore, the boys were still talking and the old man was still listening and drinking. Mary regarded them with wonder. She knew that when ordinary men drank so much their tongues began to stumble and grow weak. But Marsh Valentine showed no effect. Perhaps his eyes were a little brighter and his color a little higher, but his hand was still as steady and as strong as steel.

Making her way to her room, Mary there took out the board that during the winter months of school served her as a desk. She produced a pencil and chewed the end of it, waiting for ideas. Of course, they came slowly. Inspirations do not spring forth like magic; if there is water in the well, it must, nevertheless, be pumped out.

There was a fragment of her uncle's writing in a corner of the room, in the flyleaf of an old book. She brought it out and studied it. If she had infinite time, she might be able to duplicate that writing easily enough, but, in the meantime, she must act with haste, and so she began to compose her epistle, writing swiftly and in a general style not unlike that of Marsh Valentine.

Dear Markle:

After you left, we talked things over. And when we'd argued it back and forth, whether it'd be better to work with you against the law, or with the law against you, we finally decided that there'd be more fun in hunting you than in being hunted with you. Besides, me and the boys all feel that if we ever got to run for cover, we don't want to do it with a skunk.

So we decided that we'd go after your scalp, Markle, and that we'd get the reward that's offered. All we can't understand is how they come to put so much money on the hide of a rat like you.

This letter is to get you ready to run. Before you've had it long, I'll be along on its heels. Do some fast thinking, and you'd better ride even faster than you think. Here's wishing you better luck than I think you're going to have.

~ Marsh Valentine

She regarded this letter with the greatest pride. It was very much as her uncle would have spoken, if he felt violently upon any subject. And what the effect would be upon Markle she could surmise vividly enough when she recalled the hideous face and the animal eyes of the little outlaw.

The second letter, however, presented far greater difficulties. She had heard Markle speak only a few words. As for his handwriting, she had not the slightest conception what it might be. All had to be created from nothing; the storm had to be summoned into a sky of the purest blue. Finally she wrote in a pudgy, heavy hand:

Dear Valentine:

I've thought it over since I seen you, and I've talked it over with some of my men. Seems like I didn't know much about you. They tell me that you've got fat and lazy, and that you ain't worth much in a fight. If that's the way of it, you ain't going to be no good to me. You can stay at home and sleep. I won't be calling for you.

A couple of the boys, though, have a grudge ag'in' you. They're playing poker now to see whether or not they'll go down and clean up on you and your two kids.

This is just to let you know.

Markle

The more she regarded this second letter, the more pleased was Mary. She was confident that she had struck a note that would start the inflammable nature of her uncle into a fire of rage. And once that fire was kindled, he could not help but wish the death of Markle. It only required that the message should be brought to him before he went to bed and before the exciting tales, that his sons were telling to him, had lost their effect through the passage of ever so slight an amount of time.

Chapter Nine

"Mary the Messenger"

She knew where Markle and his men would be hiding. For she knew the hills near the town as well as she knew the course of the river and the woods that grew along its banks. If the sheriff and his men suspected that Markle was near the town and went out to hunt for him, they would be searching along the hollows and in the obscure nooks and corners of the hills. But Mary knew well enough that the outlaw would not hide in any such sort of place. He would look for only one thing, and that would be a region where he could see a foe at a distance and be prepared either to attack or flee, according to the strength of the enemy. There was one ideal place for that location.

Far back from the town, where the hills rolled up to the size of small mountains, there was a plateau shaped like the hump upon a camel's back. There were two sharp walls to the north and to the south, precipices that a man could not mount without difficulty, and which a horse could not climb at all. But to the east and the west, the slopes were more practicable. And on the top of this plateau, as Mary was reasonably certain, the great outlaw would take up his quarters—his controlling reason would be that no one could expect him to try to find a hiding place in a spot as bare as the palm of one's hand.

He would be protected by the very unexpectedness of his location. It was too large a district to be surrounded by anything less than a regiment. And yet it was so small that a pair of lookouts could take precautions against any party attempting to steal in. Mary had often wondered why that plateau was not combed by a searching squad. Now she made the place the goal of her journey.

It meant a brisk ride, and she put the gray mare mercilessly over the road, and, where there was no road, she went a twisting way along cow paths, and, where the cow paths vanished, she struck across country in an arrow-straight flight. Up the eastern grade toward the top of the plateau she struck without the slightest slowing of her horse. If the outlaw were, indeed, in refuge in this place, he would be watched by a sentinel at the head of either end of the upper level. But if she went boldly in, she might be taken in the darkness for a member of the gang coming in, or for some friend of the gang approaching with news.

In fact, she had barely gone halfway up the slope when someone whistled from the clump of trees which stood on the top of a little knoll. She pressed on the faster. The whistle came again, and this time shrill and high pitched, as though in alarm. And this time she replied with the very phrase the whistler had used, running the notes out as fluidly as though she had practiced the air a thousand times. She rode on, swaying a little to one side in the saddle in her eagerness to watch and to hear, but there was no other sound, and it was patent that her whistle had been the appointed sign. Hastily she conned it again in her mind and whistled it in a soft rehearsal to herself. If there were a second sentinel, she would be prepared.

But, without the sign of a shadow, she reached the top of the slope, and there was the long and narrow stretch of the plateau before her, with pointed rocks thrusting up on its face, and massive clusters of trees here and there.

If the whistle down the slope had prepared her to find that her guess had been correct, she could not have dreamed that she would discover the whole camp left so open to approach. She felt something that was almost akin to shame, as she looked upon it. One good rifleman, quick on the trigger, could do much damage in this place before the remnant of the gang reached safety.

The last of a big fire burned in the center of a great circle of rocks. The glow of the half-dead embers and the reflection of the light from the polished surfaces of the rocks showed half a dozen figures asleep before the fire and the outer rim of the rocks. In fact, it was a perfect retreat. The great fire would serve to cook the food of the gang and to keep them warm at night; the immense boulders would shut away the major forces of even a storm wind; and, above all, the big rocks would keep the light from showing from the top of the plateau upon the plain beneath. They had only to take care that no smoke rose during the day. At night they could heap up as huge a pyre as they chose, for the flames could never become visible.

Suppose that Uncle Marsh had been in her place? He could have shouted an alarm, to give the outlaws a fighting chance, and then, when they bolted for cover, he could have picked off half their number.

So thought Mary, as she reined her horse on the verge of the circle of the rocks. Her own work must be just as spectacular, but of a different kind. A gust of wind tossed up half a dozen points of flame and showed her the face of Markle, as he lay asleep, and, though she had never seen him, she could recognize him at once by the descriptions which she had heard of him. For his features, as he slept, were almost as brutal as though he were waking. She sent the gray mare ahead, and the fine horse, as though realizing that a light step was necessary here, stole forward without making a sound until it stood directly by the side of the sleeping chief. Then the letter fluttered from the hand of Mary' and struck the face of Markle. At the same instant she uttered a piercing yell and touched the mare with her heels.

The result was pandemonium. Half a dozen forms rose to their feet, shouting, while the mare darted away through them, leaped through a gap in the rocks on the farther side of the circle, and was gone into the outer darkness before a single bullet had been sent after her.

Once in the open, she swung the gray sharply around and sped back along the same course by which she had climbed. A horseman grew up out of the gloom before her. She swerved the mare to one side, and, as she flattened herself along the neck of the flying animal, a bullet hissed above her. Then she was past that outer guard and shooting down the slope. Other bullets combed the air above her and about her. Behind the sentinel, who was vainly rushing after her and shooting as he went, there arose a vague hubbub. But with every moment she left that noise farther behind. The shooting ceased, and presently she was galloping beyond danger. There was nothing to accompany her, saving the wild beating of her heart and a fierce sense of exultation.

She cut back for the house of the Valentines. What remained of her work must be done very quickly, for, unless she was very mistaken, the men of Markle would be soon riding hard and fast to avenge the insult to their leader. The house was as she left it—dark, save for the one light in the one window. She made that out, and then she reached the barn and put up the gray mare. Coming back toward the house, she picked up a large rock, and to the rock she tied the letter that she had written in the name of Markle.

Pausing at the window, she looked in. There sat Uncle

Marsh, and his two sons were with him. And, facing the trio, was Lefty Kinkaid. He had argued in vain, it seemed. For the three faces were utterly hostile as they regarded him. Indeed, he was on the very point of taking his departure and had picked up his hat.

Now, or never, was the time for Mary. Straight through the window she hurled the rock. There followed a crashing of the glass of the pane and the tinkling of the broken fragments upon the floor inside. There followed the shouts of the men, also, and the deep roar of Uncle Marsh, telling Oliver to guard the front door and Jack the rear, while he himself took care of the window.

She saw and heard this much. Then she was up the drainage pipe leading to the window of her room. It was a strain even for her wiry arms and her bare, active feet, but she reached the window at last, swung herself through, and lay at last huddled beneath the bedclothes. But, since they did not immediately come up to search for her, she decided that there was a logical course open that would enable her to see with her own eyes what was going on downstairs. So she jumped up from the bed again, and sped down the stairs. At the door of the dining room she paused, yawning wide and pretending to rub the sleep out of her eyes. As a matter of fact, she was alert in every sense to what was happening before her.

Chapter Ten

"Markle Saves Mary"

When Lefty Kinkaid started for the Valentine house, it had
been half unwillingly, half in rage. He felt that he had been
bewitched by a child, and he was accordingly half bewil-
dered and half furious. His fine mare was gone. Upon the
back of the horse, that had given him his safety for all
the period during which he had been a stranger to the law,
the girl had ridden away, and here he was left almost as
helpless as a fish out of water.

Having committed himself so far in the ways of folly,
there seemed nothing left but to march ahead in the same
course. So he went on to the house of the Valentines. There
his reception was typical of Uncle Marsh. He was greeted
heartily and cordially, although they had never been good
friends before the killing that had made Lefty flee for his
life. He was given the most comfortable chair. Food was
warmed for him by Oliver and Jack, while Uncle Marsh

poured forth the drinks. Even when he had finished what he could eat of the meal that they placed before him, there was still not a question asked about his errand to them that night, nor was there a word about his wanderings during the period since Uncle Marsh had last seen him.

The courtesy of Marsh Valentine had rough edges, but his heart was right. There could be no doubt of that. And something fine under an odd exterior—the same thing that Lefty had sensed in Mary Valentine—it seemed to him was in her uncle. As for the two younger Valentines, they were as yet not developed enough to show their real characters, and they had wandered so far and so long that a wolfish air sat upon them and gleamed out of their eyes.

When he broached his business, Uncle Marsh said not a word. He was busy looking down to his clasped hands in his lap, where he was twining and untwining his thick fingers. But the two sons were black of brow at once. They pushed back their chairs a little. Their scowls dwelt heavily upon him, and it seemed to Lefty Kinkaid that their big hands were lingering suspiciously near their guns. At last Jack could endure it no longer.

"Looks to me," he said, "like it would be a damn' strange thing for a Valentine to foller the lead of any other man. What work *we* got to do, I guess could be done with our own planning and our own hands. Ain't I right, Dad?"

Marsh grunted.

"Ain't I right?" asked Jack more eagerly. "You ain't going to listen to what this here Kinkaid has got to say?"

This was sufficiently irritating to have brought a sharp response from Lefty, but, since that fatal day on which he had given loose rein to his temper, he had kept it carefully under check. He checked it now. Moreover, the heavy voice of the father rolled over his son's remarks at once.

"Shut up, Jack," he said. "You dunno nothing. And the talking that needs to be done, I guess that I can do it."

Now he turned upon Kinkaid. "The way I size it up, Kinkaid," he said, "you want to clean up on Markle and his gang so's you can get back in good standing with the sheriff. Is that it? Has old Aldridge got under your skin a bit?"

"I'm afraid of the law," admitted Lefty with such frankness that the two younger men started. "Besides, I want what the law won't let me have."

"All right," said Marsh Valentine, "you would get a pardon out of cleaning up Markle's gang . . . but what would we get? Fame?"

"Fame," said Lefty, nodding. "You'd be knowed all over the range. . . ."

"As the gents that Lefty Kinkaid used for cleaning up Markle."

"I'm not the leader. I'll work under your orders, Valentine. All I want is a chance to tackle this job along with you and Oliver and Jack."

Marsh growled, but it was evident that he was a little moved by this thought.

"I used to have a lot of fool ideas," he declared, "when I was a kid. But now that I'm pretty close to being called a man, I ain't hankering after no fame with a bunch of lead inside of my skin. No, thank you, Lefty!"

"There's a better reason than that," said Lefty. He had saved the vital pressure only for the case of the strictest necessity. He saw that necessity now, and reluctantly he used his last weapon. "Since Jack and Oliver ran amuck," he said, "how many folks trust you or them? How many are just waiting for you to make one little slip before they jump on you? If anything goes wrong within a hundred miles, ain't you going to be hunted and shadowed like three crooks? What I'm offering you is the same thing I'm trying for myself . . . and that's a chance to get all squared before the law."

"Curse the law!" roared Marsh Valentine, and beat upon the table before him. "Curse the law! I don't need somebody patting me on the back to tell me what's right and what's wrong! The law has got along without me, and now I'll get along without the law!''

There were heavy growls of approval from his sons; their hearts were already fast on the side of Markle, and they had dreaded lest their father should slip from his first resolution to fight on the side of the famous outlaw. Not that they loved bloodshed and cruelty, but they *did* love adventure, and it was adventure that they expected to find when they rode at the side of the peerless leader.

It was at this point that Lefty Kinkaid gave up the battle and turned to pick up his hat. It was at this point, also, that a stone crashed through the window.

There followed a few seconds of pandemonium, during which Lefty found himself looking down the muzzle of a gun held in the hand of old Valentine—a gun that had been produced with magic speed.

"If there's something about to be double-crossed, and you're in it, you go first, Lefty," he said to his guest.

He sent his sons to guard the front and the rear of the house, and, in the meantime, he jerked the gun out of Lefty's holster. He had proceeded thus far, however, when he noted the paper tied to the rock that had been thrown through the pane of glass. He snatched it up, unrolled it, read it, and called to his boys in a voice of thunder that brought them running. It was that tableau which Mary had witnessed from the door, as she stood rubbing her eyes in pretended sleepiness. And she heard Uncle Marsh read the letter. Twice he read it. The first time rapidly, only pausing to exclaim now and again; the second time with great slowness, waiting for comments, as he completed every phrase. And the comments came in the greatest abundance. There were roars of execration from the two boys. Only Lefty was silent.

"But it ain't possible!" cried Marsh at last. "It ain't possible that I've got so old that folks should begin to talk down to me. The only thing that it looks like to me is that this letter is a joke, and that somebody must have wrote it out and just signed the name of Markle to it!''

''D'you want Kinkaid to stand around and hear all of this?'' asked Jack.

''Kinkaid and the rest of us are going on the trail of that skunk,'' said Marsh Valentine. ''What he knows don't make no difference. But is this letter square? Don't nobody know what the handwriting of Markle is like?''

He showed the letter around the room, and it was eagerly scanned. But the general opinion was that, in the absence of exact information, the handwriting was, indeed, exactly such as might be expected to come from the blunt fingers and the heavy wrist of the outlaw.

''And it's like Markle to send the letter in that way ... crashing it through the window,'' said Marsh slowly. ''There ain't any doubt about that. No, this here letter come from Markle, and now. . . . What are *you* doing down here?''

He reached the door with a stride, seized Mary by the neck, and dragged her into the light.

''I heard a bunch of shouting and a crash down here,'' said Mary, ''and I just come down here to look what might be happening.''

''Hmm,'' said her uncle. ''There's some kind of an instinct in me that tells me that you're a-lying, Mary. And you got some trouble coming ahead for you, if you have.''

''I'm telling you the honest truth,'' said Mary, shaking her head, as if to deprecate his doubt.

''Where you been?''

''In bed, of course!''

''How come you got your overalls and your shirt on? Been sleeping in them?''

''I seen her asleep in 'em,'' said Oliver, rather kindly coming to her rescue.

''Shut up,'' snapped the old man over his shoulder. ''You don't see nothing. Mary, where you been?''

''In bed.''

146

"That's a lie."

She shrugged her shoulders.

"How come you been in bed, when I can smell hoss on you? You been riding!"

She blinked. What could she invent that would satisfy the old judge?

"I'll tell you honest, Uncle Marsh."

"Fire away."

"I couldn't sleep very well. I just woke up with a bad dream in the middle of the night and couldn't go to sleep again."

"Bad dream! Bad conscience," grunted her uncle.

"Well," continued Mary, "when I seen that I couldn't get to sleep, I thought I'd have a ride. So I went out to the stable. . . ."

"How did you get downstairs, with us sitting right in here all the time?"

A precious secret must be sacrificed, now. But she gave it up instantly. "I went down the drain right outside of my window."

"Ah?" exclaimed her uncle, but he said no more.

"Then I went to the stable and caught up old Barney hoss. . . ."

"You rode Barney?"

"Yes."

"Mary, since when has Barney got gray hairs?"

She looked down. Yes, on the roll of her overalls, where they were turned up to the knee around her bare legs, there were some unlucky gray hairs from the mare.

"Now," said her uncle, curiously rather than in a passion, "how you going to get out of this hole, Mary? Where can you wriggle out?"

But Mary threw up her head suddenly. "Markle'll save me!" she said with a ring in her voice. "Listen!"

And, as she raised her head, they heard the rushing of many horses sweeping straight on through the night toward the ranch house. Sudden surmises of what this strange child might know and had done leaped into every eye. Even her uncle gave back from her. Then a yell tingled across the night air, and Marsh Valentine groaned with excitement.

"It *is* Markle!" he said, "and, now, we got our work before us!"

Chapter Eleven

"In the Angel in the House"

"It ain't possible!" cried Oliver Valentine. "Even Markle ain't got the nerve to try to rush this here house, with the village so close to it!"

"You dunno Markle," answered his father. "But I *do* know him, and I know that nothing is too much of a chance for him to take. There's four walls to this here house, and there's only three men. Maybe that's one thing he figures on. He'll come at us from all four sides and get through on one of 'em . . . unless we can count on you, Lefty Kinkaid?"

Kinkaid wrung Marsh Valentine's hand. "I'm here to the finish," he said. "Let me have the gun again."

It was passed to him, and Valentine's stentorian voice assigned the places for each of the combatants. There was a man for the front door and the rear, and there was another for a window on each of the other sides of the house. Then he caught Mary by the shoulder, as she strove to dart out of the room.

"Where are you going?" he shouted.

"To get to the village and find the sheriff," she said.

"To bring help? Forget the sheriff! There never was a crook and a gang of crooks in the world that could beat four honest men."

And Mary, numb with wonder and with happiness, stood back and smiled up at him. No matter if it were her work, and if the end of that work brought destruction upon the Valentines. In the meantime, it was also her work that had roused them to the truth and made them see that it was better to die as honest men than to live as rogues. And her own blood felt cleaner and her heart stronger.

Then the storm broke suddenly, as the thunder shower sometimes drops out of a black sky, one or two distant rumbles and, then, a rattling flood of water, crashing upon the roof. A chorus of yells besieged the house and poured around it from every side. Then guns began to crack, as volleys of shots smashed through the house. And all the time came that wild Indian yelling, that was characteristic of the Markle gang, as though they wished to give proof that they were savages, devoid of the kindness of other men. She had heard of their battle cries, but she had never been able to conjure up a mental image of such wolfish wails proceeding from human throats. They stopped her heart and made her nerves jangle. And she knew that, as those cries swung down over the village, the horror of them would stop the hearts of the villagers, just as they had stopped hers. The crowd of rescuers would assemble slowly, very slowly, and push at a snail's pace up the slope to the house of the Valentines. Before they arrived, the torrent would have washed away the defenders and left them dead.

She crouched in the dining room and listened. She found herself saying over and over: "It's terrible . . . I'm afraid! It's terrible! I'm afraid!"

But she was not afraid, and it seemed to her more glorious than terrible. Indeed, she could not feel what she expected to feel. All of her young life she had loved thunderstorms. When the sky was black and the rain whipped down and the thunder burst in drenching waves of noise and the lightning ripped the fabric of the world in twain, then she was happiest, spurring a frightened horse down a wild mountain road, alone. Or, she would stand still, with her hands flung out, palms up, and her face turned upward. And this breaking of the battle was like the breaking of the storm, except that men became more wonderful and more beautiful to her than the powers of the elements.

It was the central room of the house and the largest, this room in which she stood, and from it she could look through the open doors and see each of the defenders at his work. For lights there were small flashes, like the leap of miniature thunderbolts, with this sinister distinction: the lightning was aimed blindly at the whole round earth, but the bullets were impelled by cunning hands.

And by those darting tongues of fire it seemed to Mary that she saw enough to read the character of each of the fighters. There was Marsh Valentine, walking steadily up and down past two windows. He carried a long-barreled rifle, that spoke more seldom than the weapons of any of the others. But when it did speak, it appeared to Mary that one of the assailants must surely fall. And there were Jack and Oliver, shouting and laughing and raging at their work and calling to their father, who called back to them with a voice even louder than theirs. They were like demons enjoying a scene in hell.

But there was not a sound from Lefty Kinkaid. He had no rifle. Instead, he had taken another revolver to be used with his own gun. He had one in either hand, and he slunk from window to window along his side of the house, a form as secret and as deadly as a hunting panther. The crackle of his weapons seemed lost in the louder roaring of the rifles of the other three, and so he appeared to be shooting silently. She wondered at him. He had seemed strangely gentle before. Now he seemed more terrible than all the others.

It was amazing that with three such defenders the assailants could endure the fire for a single instant. There could not be more than seven or eight of them, and enough bullets had already been fired by expert hands to have laid low three dozen fighters. Yet still there seemed greater and greater need of battle. And she remembered the handicaps of the defenders. They themselves fought through doors and windows, and every door and window was, therefore, made a target by the approaching outlaws. But the men in the house had nothing to guide their own shots. In the blackness beyond the house the enemy was invisible, except for the occasional flashes of guns. But these were illusory lights that misled, rather than guided, their aims.

Whatever happened on the outside, the roar of their guns did not diminish. But there was a sudden cry from Jack Valentine. He reeled back into the dining room, holding his right hand with his left. He seemed infuriated, not in pain.

"Any other place but this," he shouted. "Right through the right forearm . . . and me with no chance to handle a gun now!" He sank into a chair and shook his left hand at the roar of the battle. "Curse them," he said. "If I can get this one hand on one of 'em . . . if I could sink my fingers in the fat throat of that Markle, I'd tear his windpipe out!"

"Gimme your hand," said Mary. "You gotta have it fixed up."

"What d'you know about putting on a bandage . . . in the dark?"

"Shut up . . . stop talking. You're bleeding mighty fast. Gimme that arm and keep quiet!"

She did not know herself, but wondered at the firm-nerved soul that had taken possession of her body. She took the hand, felt the hot crimson sweeping down it. She used Jack's knife and with it slashed strips from his shirt. These she bound around his arm.

"It ain't much," she told him, as she worked. "It must have been a rifle bullet. A revolver slug would have tore you up pretty bad, Jack. But the rifle bullet just slipped right through and didn't do you much harm to speak about."

She finished the bandage.

"Go sit over there ag'in' the wall," she commanded, pushing his great bulk before her, as he rose from the chair. "Sit right down here with your back ag'in' the wall, and . . . here's your rifle." She ran back and brought it. The barrel was so hot that it singed the skin of her hands. Yet she loved that pain. It was a small contribution which she could make to the great cause, that little agony of the burned hands.

"Take this here gun and balance it across your knees. You can't fight steady, but, if they bust in, you could get in one shot . . . you could kill one of 'em, Jack!"

"Mary . . . you're a wonder. If you was a man, you'd be the best ever."

She had hardly turned from him, when Oliver Valentine fell with a groan. He had run for an instant to the front of the house to take the place of his brother, quitting his own station for an instant. And he had hardly arrived before the door when he was felled, as though there were stationed opposite that place of vantage a destroyer able to see in the dark. Mary raced to Oliver.

"They got me," he gasped to her. "They got me good."

"Where, Oliver? Where?"

"You wouldn't understand. It ain't nothing. I ain't whining, am I? Run along, Mary. Get down into the cellar. What d'you mean by being up here where one of them bullets might. . . ." He stopped with a stifled groan.

"Where? Where?" she begged him, as she fumbled at his body. She had never known before how she loved that great, rough-handed fellow. He had really taught her the fine points of riding, and for that alone she would owe him a deathless gratitude. She found the place where his shirt was wet with crimson. He winced at her touch.

"Leave me be," he told her. "There ain't nothing can be done for me. It landed me square in the breast."

"But here's where it came out. Your side is all soaking with crimson, Oliver. That slug must have glanced off the ribs, and come around out here. It don't amount to nothing. You see, all you need is patching."

"All I need is water. Say, Mary, I'm burning up inside."

"I've heard 'em tell why. It's the loss of the blood that gives you a fever inside. But you'll be a pile better right *pronto*. Wait till I get this plugged up, and then you can have all the water that you can drink."

"God bless you, honey."

"Just help me by trying to lift yourself when I say, so's I can get the bandage around you."

While she spoke, she was ripping his shirt away. His naked chest, hot, rippling with giant muscles, was under her hands. If God could give her a sense of touch equal to sight for one minute, she might stop that flow of crimson.

In an instant, she was at work, and he obediently shifted the bulk of his body at her command. So the bandage was made and drawn taut with all her strength, until he groaned and groaned again under the agony of it. Then, as she made the knot fast, certain that her work had failed, but still with a blind hope that the flowing of the crimson might have been checked a little, she heard a shout from his lips, a shout echoed by Jack against the wall.

She turned and saw the huge bulk of Uncle Marsh, lighted by the flashes of his rifle that he was still blindly firing through the window, stagger back into the center of the room and crumple upon the floor.

Chapter Twelve

"Heroes All"

It was like the fall of Atlas who had upheld their little world from destruction. Oliver began to drag his half-wrecked body toward his father. Jack threw away the rifle, as though mere weapons could be of no more use, now that the keystone of the arch had fallen.

"Get away from me," snarled Marsh Valentine. "They've drilled me clean through the right leg. It ain't nothing. I can still sit and fight 'em. Get back to your guns and start shooting. I can bandage myself. I'll wring necks for this!"

But, for all his defiance, the battle was plainly lost to the defenders. All that Mary could wonder about and wish for was the coming of succor from the village. Certainly they must have heard the sounds of the firing long before, and they must have begun gathering a mob of armed men to go to the assistance of their companion on the hill. And yet, she remembered two things with a sinking heart. After all, the battle had only lasted a few minutes, and those men in the village, brave though they were, would not hurry so fast to the assistance of men in such repute as the Valentines. There was still time, there was still ample time for the enemy to discover the weakness of the defense and to rush the place. For here were walls undefended upon three sides, and Marsh Valentine was down for the time being. He must bandage that leg before he could fight, otherwise, it simply meant bleeding to death.

"It's all Kinkaid, now," said Marsh Valentine. "It's all up to him and what he can do."

Kinkaid was doing his best, and his best was a very great deal. He squatted in the dining room, at a point where his revolvers could sweep every room of the lower floor of the house. If the enemy could gain the upper story, the game was over, of course. In the meantime, from the central vantage point, Kinkaid might be able to keep off the assailants for the time being. But in the position which commanded the other rooms, he was also exposed to a torrent of lead that, entering the house from every angle, swept across it toward the center. Hard-shooting rifles whipped their slugs through the flimsy walls of the shack, as though they were paper.

Something stung the throat of Mary. She touched her breast—red was running from a wound. It was not serious, but it would mark her for life. She had run in from the kitchen with water for Oliver, when she heard a voice wail from the outside of the house.

"Close in! Close in! You fools, have I got to do it all? They're almost finished!"

That was Markle. No other human throat could have given utterance to sounds so beast-like, so compact with horrible desire to destroy.

There was an answering shout. Surely, the shout came from twenty throats. Then a smashing volley. No, it was not one discharge, but a concentration of gun power from many hands, all working at rapid fire. With this, Kinkaid sank to the floor; the last of the defenders was down.

Mary raced up to Kinkaid, and dropped to her knees beside him. "You've got the say," she said. "You're the last to go down. If you say the word, I'll tell 'em that we've surrendered!"

"Get away from me," groaned Kinkaid and swayed to his knees. "Get away and grab two guns ... these things ... they're empty, and my cartridges are gone. Firing at shadows. Oh, for one glimpse of a target, and then I'll show 'em!"

Mary's brain went numb with joy in his courage. She turned half blindly. She found Oliver. From his holsters she carried back his two revolvers. Poor Oliver. He was lying at the side of his father, reaching out a hand to touch Marsh Valentine. Pray heaven, that he was not done for. But with the new guns in his hand, she heard a faint moan of joy from the lips of Kinkaid.

"Where are you hurt?" she said to him. "Let me try to bandage...."

"You little fool! Get away from here. The bullets are coming too fast in this place."

"They'll murder you, Lefty."

"It's for her, Mary. And if they get me, you'll tell her that it was for her sake?"

"Yes, yes!"

"God bless you, honey. If you were a man, you'd be worth a million."

The very words that someone else had said to her on this wild night. Who it was she could not for the instant remember. Leave him here? She could have laughed at the thought. He was still swaying a little upon his knees, but she knew without asking that it was not weakness, but the battle fury that swung him back and forth.

Something was in the doorway. Yes, they were charging

toward the house, yelling. A hundred fiends were shrieking, as they raced toward the old house, and there was someone who had leaped into the doorway.

"Ah!" She heard Lefty gasp the word with satisfaction, and she knew what it meant. This was the real target for which he had wished. Here it was, full before his eyes. Only a target for an instant, however, and then it swerved into darkness, but that instant had been enough. Lefty had located his mark, and, as the darkness inside the door swallowed the figure, he fired. A gun flashed twice in response—once at breast height, and once again from the level of the floor. There were the sound and the shock of a heavy body that had crashed down. The gun flashed no more. Something told Mary that yonder outlaw, who had died shooting, would never again pull a trigger.

Lefty had swerved around. He was facing the stairs. What he saw, she could not dream. All was deep dark to her. But he fired, and there was a yell, then the thundering fall of an inert body down the steps. It struck a chair in the room. The chair was turned to a limp wreck. The body revealed a man's length beyond, and then it lay without a quiver.

Two were gone. How many more? Then a voice, somewhere in the house—somewhere not far away—was crying: "Close in! There's only one of 'em. Blow him to bits!"

It was Markle again! It was that same tremendous, animal wail. But where was he? The voice seemed to press in from every direction upon them. It beat against them like a hundred hands of fear in the darkness. And Mary saw Kinkaid buckle closer to the floor with a gasp. He was afraid, just as fear had taken her by the throat, so it had taken him. A cold perspiration of shame for him stood upon her forehead. It was worse than death to find fear in such a man as Lefty Kinkaid.

It was only the flinching of an instant, however. The shadowy form of Kinkaid rose again. She saw the dim form of the guns glimmering in his hands. And now, in the parlor and rushing straight toward them, she made out a squat, bulky figure. It was Markle, she knew instantly. A little angry tongue of flame darted out. A gun boomed that seemed louder than the report of other guns, and Kinkaid went down, as though a weight had crushed him to the floor.

"He's down!" thundered Markle. "We've got 'em! Lights! Finish 'em all!"

He could see in the dark, then?

But there was a stir at her feet. It was Kinkaid turning with an effort upon his side. A gun spat from his hand, and it was answered by a sharp howl from Markle. Yet it seemed incredible to her that the charge of the squat form could have been stopped. Instinctively she knew that the adroit fighter, who had brought down Jack and Oliver, was the leader of the gang. But yonder he was, on the floor like Kinkaid, but now pouring forth a double stream of bullets. Something stung her again, this time on the shoulder. But she felt no desire to flee. There was only a thrust of hot joy that proved to her that the bullets of the leader were flying wild. She saw Kinkaid writhe still higher. She saw the gleam of his gun, as he steadied himself. Oh, nerve of iron that could brace him to take time for deliberate aim in the face of that avalanche of bullets.

The gun exploded. There was a roar of agony in the black darkness, and the shadow that was Markle disappeared on the black floor. And then, in the great distance, so it seemed to Mary, there were voices calling. Did she recognize the call of the mighty sheriff? But what she did hear with certainty was the calling of other voices in the house itself.

"They're cutting us off. Get back to the hosses!"

Now the trampling of feet began. So much she heard. Or, rather, it was as though a great hand that had been supporting her was now removed, and she was allowed to slump down. She stumbled. Her mind was blacker than the darkness around her.

"Lefty," she murmured, "I'm kind of sick. I . . . I'm dying, Lefty!"

But it was only a swoon. When she wakened, the dream of darkness was gone. She found herself lying on a bed in the best room in the best house in town. And beside her bed was Nancy Pembroke. She watched Nancy with a strange and quiet interest. It seemed to her that she could read a whole long story in the face of the teacher.

"Miss Pembroke," she said at last.

There was a cry of happiness from Nancy. Her gentle arms went around the body of her patient.

"Miss Pembroke, I guess Lefty pulled through all right."

"He'll be walking in a week."

"And Uncle Marsh and . . . ?"

"All three of them are going to get well. And the whole town knows that they are heroes now, and not simply black sheep, dear. You've opened the eyes of everyone."

"Me? I didn't do nothing. I just gave 'em a chance," said Mary.

"Oh, my dear!" cried Nancy Pembroke. "But *I* know the truth, and so does Lefty. *You* wrote the letters, and *you* carried them. Lefty guessed it first. And, oh, Mary, when you grow up, you'll be a woman in a million!"

"These left-handed gents," said Mary, "they sure got a funny way of thinking things out, eh?" And she added after a time: "Say, Miss Pembroke, have you got the makings?"

SAFETY McTEE

This short novel first appeared in Street & Smith's *Western Story Magazine* (8/25/23). McTee is a gunman who has earned his moniker because he has, in his way, always played it safe in gun fights. But more happens than that, when McTee develops a friendship with those he has bested and even falls in love with the niece of a man whom he has wounded. As with the other short novels in this collection, "Safety McTee" is published here in paperback for the first time.

Chapter One

"A Typical McTee Fight"

The second time McTee won on his own deal, the four others in the game began to notice his luck. But when he won the third time, it was a little too remarkable to escape notice. The other players suspected that he was cheating, but they were unable to detect him in a single crooked move. He would bet with as much assurance upon three of a kind as upon a full house, and his invariable audacity with every hand left them in the dark as to when he was bluffing and when he held the cards. In the first six or seven hands he had scored so heavily that he had gathered in the major portion of the cash which was afloat in that quintet. He could afford to sit back and float through the game. There was no chance that he could lose much of his winnings, for, when the game started, he had announced that he could only stay with it for a matter of two hours. And the two hours was up.

If it had been any other man, his singular fortune would

have produced a gun argument on the spot. But Safety McTee was too well known, and no one but a fool cared to take liberties with him in the way of free speech or free manners.

He was nicknamed Safety not because of the uniform gravity of his manners and caution in his affairs, but because he was famous for knowing how to proceed to the limit of danger without actually encroaching upon the brink of a fall. Such was the repute of McTee that, though he was known to have been in many gun fights, yet in every one of these the other man had given the offense. In short, he was one who strikes without legal risk to himself. Safety was practically a newcomer. All that was in circulation about him was his nickname and the explanation that with a gun he was the same as death guaranteed.

But his gray eyes were as big, as steady, and as frankly bright as those of the most harmless man who ever stepped. He was well past thirty, but he looked five years younger, so well was he preserved. His features were cut as though from stone, and chiseled by a master; his six feet and more of sinewy brawn were cared for as the most self-respecting athlete would have cared for himself. And, on the whole, he presented the perfect picture of a successful young rancher who has fought his way up and is still capable of battle, but all in honesty, all in frank manliness.

Of the four at the table with him, now, there was not one who took his losses easily. But he who took them the hardest was actually the one who had lost the least. This was a stripling in his early twenties with a boyish, eager face, now overcast with guilty shadows. Plainly he had not played often. His stakes had been raked nervously. When he won, he was bright with elation. When he lost, he was gloomy. In another hour every man at the table would be able to read his face.

Apparently he had lost almost the last of his money on

the final deal of Safety McTee. But he still sat in the game, trying in a small way to regain his lost coin. Also, he was extremely reminiscent. And suddenly he flashed up at big McTee: "Ain't you the McTee that used to be up to Larsen way?"

"I disremember," said McTee with perfect assumption of carelessness. "I'm taking three," he added to the dealer.

But the youngster would not be put off the trail. "Didn't you never meet up with a man named Rube Kenshaw?"

"Rube Kenshaw? Rube Kenshaw?" murmured Safety. "I dunno that I place that name."

"Try again!" exclaimed the youngster. "Wasn't it Kenshaw that lost five hundred dollars to you playing blackjack one evening?"

He pointed an accusing finger at McTee across the table. It was enough to have made another man fight, but McTee did not change color or voice.

"Maybe I won five hundred from a man named Kenshaw. It ain't likely, though. I don't often play."

"But," cried the young fellow, who was addressed as Bill Donnelly, "if you're the man that Kenshaw played with, you've done more card playing than anything else in your life."

It was going a little too far. Somebody hissed a soft warning to Bill Donnelly. The other three at the table had pushed back their chairs a trifle. Donnelly himself seemed to realize in a flash that he had talked too much. He hesitated, coughed, and passed a hand across his forehead, looking modestly down to his cards.

But a little cruel smile played on the lips of Safety McTee. He was not of a mind to let the matter rest where it was. Not by any means. The smile vanished from his lips, and his face grew thunderously black.

"Will you say that over again, and say it loud enough for me to hear what you're saying?"

His voice passed boldly through the big room. It beat

against the ear of a score of others who lounged here and there or sat at the tables. And they glanced sharply around. There was no mistaking that tone of the angry man, the man who feels that he has been injured.

Poor young Donnelly felt that battery of eyes playing upon him, and to him it meant death. He remembered now that it was too late. Kenshaw had told him a great deal about this handsome McTee, with his strange gray eyes and his black hair. This was one who never failed with his weapons. As for Donnelly, the hard work in the mine had stiffened his fingers. Whatever skill he had with a gun was not for a quick draw. As a hunter he was one of the best. As a man fighter he was worse than useless. And Donnelly knew all of his own weakness as well as the strength of his opponent.

It was death, then. At this distance such a man as McTee could not miss a vital spot. And Donnelly looked across the room to a spot of sunshine on the floor. A cat was curled up in that shaft of gold, a black cat, twitching her ear in the delicious comfort of the warmth and perhaps dreaming of tinned fish. How beautiful it was to live, if only as that dumb beast. But to leave the life of a young man in the very blossom of his time—to give up the girl who had let him hold her hand and whisper at her ear the week before at the dance, to wake no more when the sun rolled over the mountain tops—all of this to be done away with by the touch of a piece of lead, and for what?

He stared blankly at McTee. He saw that the black look had turned to an expression of contempt. He glanced hastily around the room. Yes, upon still other faces there were sick looks of disgust. No wonder. He knew suddenly that he had been gaping at McTee, his terror written upon his face. No, a thousand times better to die than to be ashamed. He leaped to his feet and snatched the revolver from his holster.

"I called you crooked. . . ."

He swung the gun at the head of McTee, but, before he

could fire, a gun exploded beneath the table. McTee had simply tilted up the bottom of his holster and fired the gun through it. And Donnelly pitched to one side. He had been shot neatly through the thigh of the leg.

Chapter Two

"Shorty Starts Mischief"

No one could possibly have asked for his arrest. He had simply been insulted in a public place by a young hothead who had jerked out a gun and tried to shoot him down. McTee had luckily been able to get rid of a bullet sooner, though there was a score of witnesses to the truth that he had not stirred a hand until the gun of the other was actually out of its holster.

But, although these were the facts, everyone was aware of the truth behind the facts. McTee had planned that shot beneath the table. It was for that reason he sat a little to one side in his chair. The attitude of apparent carelessness had, as a matter of fact, simply prepared the way for the bullet that he was eventually to fire. And here he had another victim to his credit, and there was still not so much as a scratch upon the strong body of McTee. The town rumbled its anger. And in half an hour after the shooting scrape a hundred rumors concerning Safety McTee had been gathered, and his history—a little more lurid than the truth—had been patched up. It was then seen what manner of man he was. It was then declared softly upon every side that there should be a new set of laws framed for such men as McTee. It was even suggested that they should organize a lynching party to roll him in tar, feather him well, and then string him up until he was well nigh choked.

However, nothing passed beyond the stage of talk. There was something infinitely disconcerting in the thought of that long-barreled Colt, so heavy in the hand, but so delicately light in the expert fingers of McTee. If people were to rush that gun, they could not escape without the loss of a life for every bullet in its chambers. These quieting thoughts caused the talk of tar and feathering to die away without action. But, in the meantime, there was something more to talk about. And again it was Safety McTee who was the center of the conversations.

McTee had sat in at another game of cards that afternoon, and the report was that he had been heavily trimmed and had lost most of the money that he had won in the morning for the simple reason that he had been scalped by a pair of professionals. The result was that Safety McTee was in far from the best humor and looked about for a means of venting his spleen.

This required the laying of plans. Neither of the two professionals could be tempted into a quarrel of any kind with McTee. They laughed in his face when his talk became irritating, and then they departed with the spoils of the war. And McTee had to lay his plans for building up another enemy and another quarrel into which he could enter as the defendant and not as the aggressor.

What he did was to say that he understood that Bill Donnelly's brother, Jack, had come to town with him, as they were both to buy provisions for their father, who remained at their mine in the Cruikshank Mountains. And since Jack was in town, he would doubtless require from him, Safety McTee, a very exact explanation of the manner in which his brother had come to be hurt, and, in that case, Safety declared that he would be only too glad to oblige the gentleman.

But this was rather too obvious. Everyone who heard these remarks understood that Safety was simply working up more business for his gun, and they were not tempted to carry the message to honest Jack Donnelly. There was one exception to this, however. Shorty Crew was a poor devil who had been born with a curve in his back that never could be straightened. When he attempted to work as a boy, he had merely bent himself all the more. And he remained twisted and looking more than half ready to break to the end of his life. He could not work. He lived upon the charity of the town, and like many invalids he repaid the kindness of the townsfolk by taking to heart all the malice in the world. He was the village gossip. No woman could carry such a fund of information as he. All of Shorty's gossip was of the sort that had to be whispered in corners or else told with frequently lifted eyebrows and evil smiles and cruel insinuations. To the women he was a bitter luxury. To the men he was simply detestable. But what the women wanted they retained, and Shorty still existed in the town because nobody would stoop to the mean work of ousting the hunchback from the place.

It was Shorty who, on the outskirts of the group, heard the remark. In an instant he was off to carry the tidings to the victim. He found Jack Donnelly properly at the bedside of his brother, and he drew the big fellow outside.

"Have they told you what's happened?" he asked.

"What's happened about what?" asked Jack. "You don't mean to say that anything has happened to poor old Dad up to the mine?"

For the old man had been left there alone.

"I dunno," said Shorty. "Maybe there's something wrong

at the mine, too, for all I know. But what I been hearing is the way that Safety McTee has been talking.''

"What's he been talking about? And who has he been telling it to?"

"He's been telling it to everybody. Seems that folks expect that you should do something because McTee shot Billy."

"Me do something?"

"They say that if you was down, Billy wouldn't have rested until he'd tried his best to get back at the gent that downed you. They say that you ain't acting hardly brotherly."

There was a long pause. "You mean that I ought to start for McTee . . . with a gun?"

"*I* don't mean nothing," said Shorty. "*I* ain't suggesting anything. I only know what the talk is, and I thought that maybe you'd ought to hear it."

"But I ain't any gunfighter. Billy is twice the man with a gun than I am, and, if he couldn't do nothing with McTee, I'd just be throwing bullets away trying to tackle him. Ain't that clear? Ain't that clear, Shorty?"

"It's clear to *me*," said Shorty. "All I'm telling you is what the others think. I thought that maybe. . . ."

"Sure, I'm glad to know, but what in the devil can I do, Shorty?" Perspiration was standing upon the forehead of the unlucky fellow.

"I ain't any judge," said Shorty, "and I ain't here to give you no advice. But the way that McTee is talking is enough to make you sick inside!"

"What does he say?"

"That he's had his share of fighting before this, but that he never before seen the time when he could lick two men with one slug out'n his gun."

"Does he say that?" groaned Jack.

"That's the way he's talking. It ain't no way right and fair, is it? Some of the boys have been answering up and telling him that you're just busy taking care of Billy, and that when you got a free hand you'll come and see to him plenty.''

"Have they been saying that?''

"That's what they been saying, or words that mean the same thing.''

Jack groaned again and struck his big hands together.

"It looks like I got to go and face him,'' he muttered. "But what will Dad do when Billy is laid up and I'm . . . gone? What will poor old Dad do?''

"I dunno about your dad. I'm just telling you what the boys have. . . .''

"Damn you and the rest of the boys, and now get the devil out and lemme be here alone. I got to think.''

"That's gratitude,'' whined Shorty. "I come all this way and tell a gent something that's for his own good, and this is the way that I get an answer. Dog-gone me, if it don't discourage a gent from treating other folks like white men!'' And he shambled away.

But ten minutes later, Jack Donnelly had finished his thinking and had begun to act. He strapped on a gun. And the weight was unfamiliar at his hip. For when they were working at the mine, it was always Billy who did the hunting. The hands of Jack were accustomed only to the tools of the mine. The shooting was left to his younger brother. Nevertheless, he put on the gun and the belt and started down the street. On the verandah of the hotel he found Safety McTee and a dozen others enjoying the warmth of the late afternoon. He strode up the steps and confronted the gunfighter.

"McTee,'' he said, "I been hearing stories about what you been saying about me!''

"Me?'' said McTee softly. "Partner, I ain't been talking about you.''

"You lie!'' said Donnelly, and grasped the butt of his gun.

There was a gasp from the bystanders, who drew away from the vicinity of the two.

"That's a mighty strong word," pursued the placid voice of McTee.

"A mighty true word."

"Looks like you come down here to pick trouble with me, Donnelly. But I ain't a trouble maker or taker, if I can get out from under. All I ask is to be let to sit right here in peace. I sure hope that you ain't going to pick on me for any trouble, Donnelly."

"McTee, I ain't got no time to waste. I've come down here to call you a murdering, black-hearted hound, and I'm standing right here and telling it to your face!"

McTee rose from his chair.

"I'm going inside," he said. "I ain't here to do a killing or be killed."

He had hardly made a step when Donnelly's hand fell on his shoulder and whirled him around. "Get your gun," rasped out Donnelly, and tugged forth his own.

His gesture was like the futile, pawing stroke of the amateur boxer compared with the lightning thrust of a trained pugilist. Into the fingers of McTee whirled the long and heavy Colt. Before the gun of Donnelly was in the air, that of McTee had spoken, and Jack gasped, sagged to his knees, and then rolled upon his face and lay still.

Chapter Three

"A Journey into Foothills"

He was not dead. The sheriff brought the news of that when he called upon McTee the next morning. But he was badly hurt, and it would be a month before he could walk.

This was the first part of the sheriff's talk, and it was in answer to the gently voiced inquiry of Safety McTee. His second part had to do with McTee himself, and the other townsfolk. They had become a little restless, he said, and it would be the wise part for McTee to drift out of the town that morning before the talk gathered to a head in action.

"But," said McTee, "what have I done?"

"You ain't done nothing, of course," he said. "You ain't been anything in this here town but a peace-loving gent that has had a little trouble pushed onto you. You and me know that, McTee, but there's others in this here town that don't figure it out the same way. I'm talking to you for your own good."

"Thanks," said McTee, "but I ain't ready to move on."

"Why not? There ain't going to be any more business for you around here."

"What sort of business?"

"I guess you got some idea."

"I ain't here on business," replied McTee. "I'm here taking a rest. My nerves have got all busted up lately. All I want to do now is to sit here plumb quiet and rest my eyes on the mountains and the beautiful girls in this here town, Sheriff."

The sheriff grinned back in spite of himself. "You're a queer gent, Safety."

"Yes," said Safety, "there ain't many around these parts that like a quiet life as much as I do."

"I suppose that you've filed a couple more notches on the butt of your gun?"

"Me? What for?"

"Ain't you dropped two more? By the way, I'd sort of like to see that gun of yours."

Without a word McTee handed it to him. And it was notched, indeed, but only in five places, where notches had been cut into the wood.

"What are *these* for," asked the sheriff. "Are these for the *dead* ones?"

"Them are finger holds," said McTee, and looked the sheriff squarely between the eyes. And there was something disconcerting in that glance, so that the sheriff, though he was one of the bravest men in the world, could not help looking hastily away.

"But coming back to business," he said, "don't forget my advice."

"Thanks. I got a good sound memory. But I'd sure hate to go away before I'd had a chance to talk to all my new friends in this here place."

"McTee, this is straight talk. If you stay here till noon,

you'll be looking at the sky, and your heels ain't going to be touching the ground.''

McTee lighted his smoke and then stretched his arms above his head.

"It looks like it might turn into a real party," he declared. "And I've been missing my fun lately. But if you think that I'd better move along, I suppose that I've got to disappoint the boys, eh?''

"I dunno," said the sheriff. "There's a lot of talk. And about the middle of the morning I've got to take a ride out of town. After I'm gone, some of the boys might begin to get together and talk about stretching a rope. . . .''

"You don't need to say no more," said McTee a little sourly.

And the sheriff went about his way, contented with himself. He would have been contented enough to see McTee dangling in the air, but he did not want a lynching checked up against his term in office.

As for McTee, he went to his room and made up his pack. It was small, compact, and very light. It consisted chiefly of parched corn—at which even an Indian might have turned up his nose—bullets, and salt. In short, McTee was one of those rare adventurers who fear neither the mountains nor the desert, but will fare across them all, confident that, if he has the salt to make it palatable, his gun will bring down the meat that he needs for his campfire. He relied upon no frying pans, no coffee pots. He who lived so entirely upon the fat of the land when he was in town lived only upon the country and what it produced when he was voyaging. The salt and the corn were all that he required.

Then, with his pack made up, he stood at the window of his room in the hotel and considered the horizon. To the north and west arose the mountains, and, when he saw them, McTee remembered the mine of the Donnelly family. He had made inquiry about it after the shooting of the second brother. He learned that it was a treacherous vein that pinched out and appeared again in ground that was bitterly hard to break. For three years the three men had been toiling at it, attempting to reach farther and farther into the heart of the mountain and confident that sooner or later they would make a great strike that would enrich the entire family.

It was rather a stirring picture of faith and a miner's trust in luck. And it appealed strongly to McTee. It showed the right gambling spirit, he told himself. Besides, there was the old father left stranded, for the time being. He was expecting his two boys to come back from a week of play in town with a store of provisions. It would be a little hard, after all, if he received, instead of the supplies, only the news that they had lost their money at the gaming table and that both of them were flat upon their backs.

So McTee, with a shrug of his wide shoulders, walked down to the store with his pack slung across his back. There he made purchases of supplies that his horse could carry without distress, at the same time that it supported his own bulk. He bought a sack of cornmeal, a liberal supply of bacon, some coffee, some baking powder, some salt, and several tins of sugar. The sugar was most important, he knew. For the old fellow would find something to stew up and make a necessary variation of the diet in the mountains.

McTee despised men who needed such luxuries. He himself, when he was on the trail, lived for the trail and for nothing else. It was his coffee and tobacco, his ice cream and his cake. He merely tightened his belt when he felt a craving for the unnecessary.

With this new pack prepared he made his start for the barn.

"Starting on a trip?" asked the storekeeper cheerfully.

"I'm knitting a sweater," called McTee cheerfully over his shoulder, "to keep my dog from catching cold in the snows above timberline. So long."

In the barn he went to his horse and led the big animal out into the light. It was a great bay, as ugly as a caricature, with a long, heavy head, a long neck, and a sharp backbone. It seemed particularly ridiculous in comparison with the sleek perfection of so fine a specimen of manhood as McTee. But the latter now looked the horse over carefully, patted his neck, rubbed his ears, and slapped him playfully on the stomach.

A boy had come out from the stable. And not even a McTee could invade the spirit of a boy with awe.

"Mister," he said, "did you find that hoss, or did somebody give it to you?"

"Kid," said McTee, "what's the price of the best hoss in the barn or in the corrals?"

"There's Sam Oliver's new brown mare. They say that he paid up to eight hundred for her, and that he wouldn't take a thousand flat cash."

The awe of the child shone forth at his eyes.

"Very good," said McTee. "Well, son, if somebody was to offer me three like Sam Oliver's new brown mare, I'd rather have Bones than the whole lot of them!"

"I guess you would," admitted the boy.

"Shall I tell you why?"

"I'd sure like to hear the reason."

"Because it isn't the fast hoss that wins the race through the desert or over these here mountains. It's the hoss that hits up a good stiff jog and hangs onto it. And Bones is the one for that. And it's the hoss that can get along on a blade of grass one day and a drink when he gets in. That's the sort of a hoss that counts, son. You can lay to that! Old Bones, here, you could ride all day, and when night come along you could turn him loose and he'd find himself a meal where a rabbit would starve. That's the sort of a hoss he is."

"If the gent was hunting, or being hunted," said the boy, "I guess that would be the right sort of a hoss to have." He shook his head. "But how does he manage them big feet on a bad trail?"

"He isn't a bird," said McTee, "but he's the best imitation of a mountain sheep that you've ever seen.''

And, leaving the boy laughing behind him, he swung into the saddle on the big bay, that immediately started away at a sharp trot, not a canter. Yet, in spite of that rough gait, McTee sat the saddle with the smoothness of running water over a rough bed of rocks. And, when he stepped into action, the appearance of Bones changed at once. His big frame seemed to grow less apparent, and, instead, the long and leathery muscles played up and down his legs and across his shoulders and hips. His very head grew smaller as he carried it with a lighter grace. And the smile died out on the face of the stable boy, for he could see a clear picture of that big animal shacking away, mile after mile, through the hottest day and leaving behind him the speed of the fastest posse.

''A gent with a hoss like that don't have to be afraid of nothing,'' said the boy aloud.

Chapter Four

"*McTee Loses His Head*"

McTee headed straight up toward the gap where he had heard the Donnelly mine was located. He was not a little ashamed of his errand. But he assured himself that the place was so obscure that people would hear rather how he had shot up the two sons of the old miner and not how he had played the part of the angel of mercy and given him this stock of provisions.

When he reached the first level of the gap, narrow and rocky and with the great mountains rolling, steeply up on either hand, he saw no sign of the mine, however. There was only a wretched little shack huddled into the lee of some enormous boulders. It was inhabited, for a meager breath of smoke was rising from the old tin chimney above the house, and McTee rode up to the door, and knocked against it.

"Who's there?" called out a bass voice.

"What's the way to the Donnelly mine?" asked McTee.

"Who's there?" repeated the man inside.

"Are you deaf?" roared McTee. "Haven't you got the use of your ears? I asked the way to the Donnelly mine!"

"Be damned to you," thundered the voice, with hardly less volume. "For why should I be answering a man whose name I don't know?"

"Friend," said McTee ominously, "if I've got to come in to introduce myself, you'll wish that you'd never seen my face."

"I hate a loud talker worse'n I hate a sneak," called the man inside. "Go on with you, or I'll come out and give you a trimming, damn you! I'll learn you manners!"

McTee ground his teeth. It was against all of his principles to take the first aggressive step in a quarrel of any sort, but never before had he been badgered so effectively.

"I've asked you one civil question," he said. "Will you tell me the way to the Donnelly mine?"

"I've asked you one civil question," retorted the man inside. "Will you get away from my door and stay away?"

"I'll see you with the devil, first," bellowed McTee, and, leaning down, he struck the door heavily with his fist, a childish outpouring of vain wrath.

Then he swung down from the saddle, his revolver in his grip. He knew that he was making a great mistake, but the knowledge was tucked away in the back of his unconscious mind. Consciously he only desired to get at the owner of that heavy voice and tear him to bits. He knew, moreover, that he was not only being the aggressor, but that, by breaking into the home of another man, he was doubling his crime, whatever that might be. But such considerations could not hold him back once he had started. His wrath had as much impetus as a snowslide.

He struck the door with his shoulder, and the weight of his lunge burst the wood away from the hinges as though it was rotten. As the door went down, he had a dim view of a tall form throwing a shotgun to his shoulder. It needed quick work, then. A shotgun at that distance, loaded with buckshot or with bird shot, could not miss and, if it struck, could not fail to blow the life out of his body. He flipped up the muzzle of his revolver and fired, fired so hastily, indeed, that the bullet flew a little low, and he was about to fire again when his passion-blinded eyes saw two things. The first was that the tall man was swaying feebly from side to side, and that the shotgun was slipping from his unnerved hands. The second was that the keeper of the shack was old. He was, indeed, far past the prime of life; he must have been sixty-five if he was a day, and a long, thin, white beard straggled across the breast of his flannel shirt.

It is only justice to McTee to admit that, at that moment, he wished that the bullet had passed into his own flesh and not into that of his foeman. He cast his revolver—even that precious weapon with the five notches on the butt—into the dirt beside the open door. He leaped forward, caught the collapsing form in his big arms, and carried his victim to a bunk at the side of the room. He lowered him onto the blankets.

The bullet had cut through the thigh at almost exactly the same place where the slug had gone that had brought down young Bill Donnelly the day before. He discovered this as he slashed away the trouser leg of the wounded man. Thank heaven the hurt was not serious. But what would the world say when it discovered that the terrible McTee had actually fought with a helpless old man—a man with white hair?

He discovered, suddenly, that the world that he thought he despised was very much in his mind. He had considered himself far beyond its opinion, whether good or bad. But, now, he found himself cringing. Moreover, he had at last committed the act of open and inexcusable violence for which all his scores of enemies had been waiting. The population of whole towns would turn out for the trail when they had heard the story.

But, most of all, he winced when he saw the withered

muscles and the standing, stiff tendons of that thigh. They spoke of the dying strength of a man who had once been powerful. Age was killing his power at the root. And here was McTee, famous for his strength, striking down a helpless man! He gnashed his teeth as he worked, applying the bandage.

And, in the meantime, the old man was not silent. Yet his remarks referred not to himself.

"That's a neat trick you got of slipping your gun out of the leather," he said. "Sort of wished it out into the open, and when you touched her off, damned if you didn't shoot straight! When I was a youngster, I used to shoot pretty well myself, but I never had a knack like that."

He apparently held no malice. His comments were entirely philosophical. But this generous fashion of dealing with the encounter was simply rubbing salt into the open wound of McTee's conscience.

"Are you in a lot of pain, partner?" asked McTee anxiously.

"Was you ever shot?" retorted the old man.

"I dunno that I ever have been."

"I'm surprised to hear that. With your make-up and way of doing things, sort of looks to me like you'd've hooked up and made the acquaintance of powder and lead a long time ago. But since you don't know, I'll tell you that I been easier in my life than I am right this here minute."

"I wish to heaven," said McTee with heartfelt meaning, "that I was lying there and that you were standing here."

"Wouldn't be possible. I ain't got the strength to carry a man of your weight. What might you weigh, son?"

His gentleness was beyond belief. One might have thought that they were old friends.

"About two hundred. Is that bandage pressing too tight?"

"Nope. I'm plumb comfortable. Set down and rest yourself and show me how you made that draw again. It was the slickest thing that I ever seen.

"I didn't see your white beard," said the miserable McTee. "I swear to you, partner, that I didn't see how old you were or I wouldn't have. . . ."

"Easy! Easy," called the other. "What in the devil d'you mean? Are you starting in to pity me? Lemme tell you that I don't need no man's pity. When I get well, I'm going out to hunt you. Besides, if you hadn't got me, I'd've got you with two barrels of buckshot."

He spoke with a ferocious unction, though his voice was a trifle weaker than it had been. His eyes, too, occasionally turned sharply from one side to the other, sure sign that he was in the greatest pain.

"All right," said McTee hastily. "But I busted down your door to get at you. . . ."

"D'you think that I'm going to take you into court for this here little party? No, no, old son. I ain't that kind of coyote."

McTee breathed only a little more easily. The story would still be black against him, if ever it were noised abroad. And such a garrulous old man as this could not help but talk of such things. This was excitement enough to keep him coining anecdotes for the rest of his life.

But, still, it was not all dread of the opinion of the world, for the longer he leaned over the bunk of his victim, the better he liked the man he had dropped. The old chap was as game as any youngster. He was still smiling as he looked up into the face of McTee.

"You can lay to this," said McTee, "I'll never leave you till you're in the best of shape."

"You mean that you'll stay here and play the nurse and take care of me like I was a damned baby?"

"Do you think that I could leave you?"

"You sure will. I don't need no help. I can take care of myself. I always have, and I always will. And there's no end to that."

He stated this with a vicious little snap of his jaw to emphasize his determination.

"You can't keep me away," answered McTee smilingly, his heart warming at the courage of the old fellow.

"I'll tell you what," said the other. "I'll have plenty of care tonight. When my two boys come in, they'll go wild when they see what's happened, and they'll start trailing you!"

"Two boys?" cried McTee with a sudden thought. "Did you say two?"

"They bunk in the loft, except when the summer gets hot. Then they go outside. Sure I have two boys. Why not?"

"Donnelly!" cried McTee.

"I was meaning to ask you," said the other, "what business you had up here with me."

Chapter Five

" 'That's the Man!' "

It was a blow as heavy as it was unexpected to McTee. He
blinked at his companion and then shook his head as though
to clear away the effect of sleep from his troubled brain.

"You're Donnelly?" he echoed again.

And, looking around him, he tried to conjure up the picture of the two stalwart youths in this room. At least, this
made it certain that he would be condemned by the world.
To have shot the two boys was bad enough. But to have
deliberately hunted out the old man was too damnable. Who
could believe that his work had been anything other than
intentional?

"Sure I'm Donnelly," the veteran was saying in hot anger. "How many times do I have to tell you my name?"

"But I thought that you had a mine?"

"We have, if it ain't vanished away."

"There's no sign of a hole near this here shack. I didn't

see a hoist or anything. A mine that you've been working in for three years?''

''It's around and up the side of the mountain,'' explained Donnelly. ''There was such mighty good water down here at the spring that I figured it was better to pack ourselves up to the mine and down again than it was to pack up the water that we needed to the mouth of the mine.''

So that small mystery was explained, and McTee cursed softly and viciously to himself. Looking down to the old man, what he saw was not the time-dried features of Donnelly, but a hundred faces of his enemies, half sneering and half exultant since they saw that the time had come when they could close in upon him. And shame, too, was putting the lash upon him.

He went abruptly out of the cabin and into the open air. There he took from the big horse the pack of food and bore it into the cabin, while the bay wandered to the rear of the shack and searched there for richer pickings. He would need the best possible food and the most of it, decided McTee as he carried the provisions into the shack and sat down on an up-ended grocery box. For now would begin the longest and the hardest pursuit that he had ever commenced. He had passed through his trials before, but he had always been able to ride out of the sphere of enmity and into one in which he would be free from all except a casual danger. Now, however, his case was far, far different. Those hard-handed men of the range, as he was doubly well aware, would pass the story along and tell in town after town, county after county, and camp after camp, how Safety McTee had shot down two sons of a family and then tried to murder the helpless old father of the boys. And such a tale would drive them wild with anger. They would gather by the score to hunt him.

But worst of all, the thing he had done sapped his own moral strength. He had no courage to stand up to face the world when he was accused of such work. He must flee at once, and, yet, if he fled, he would be deserting the poor old man to certain death. He turned upon the sufferer the bitterest scowl of malice. If the old miner would only curse him to harden his heart. If he could induce Donnelly to speak in rage and in hatred to him, then all might be well, and he could persuade himself to go and let the old man lie here until he died of want. But there was not a breath of complaint from old Donnelly. His eye was as steady and as clear as the sky above the mountains. And McTee felt that his cruelty was melting out of his heart. Its passing left him with a sense of controlling weakness. He could think of a dozen of his hardy compatriots to whom such a deed as this would be less than nothing. But with himself it was different.

He went outside again, slowly. Slowly he unsaddled the big bay. And while he dragged off the mass of leather and blankets, he heard the sudden rattle of hoofs close at hand, wonderfully close. For the wind was blowing stiffly down the gap, and the rider was coming up against it. The noise of the approach had been blown in the opposite direction from McTee at the shack. The roar of the hoofs died out at the door of the cabin. And he heard a high, sweet voice of a girl crying: "Uncle Donnelly! What . . . who . . . oh, the demons, the demons!"

McTee applied his eye shamelessly to a crack between two boards, and in this fashion he was able to see her who stood on the threshold. She wore a sort of cowpuncher outfit. She was all in tan from the soft-brimmed sombrero that drooped in queer and lazy lines about her face, to the dusty boots upon her feet. He studied those boots with a swift and intense interest. They were shop made, of the finest quality, and they outlined feet so slender that it seemed to McTee both of them together would not make the mass of one of his big hands. Indeed, she was slenderly made throughout, but not weakly. No, no! She was as slim and supple as a whipstock, but there was strength in her gray eyes. It was the sort of strength he was accustomed to seeing in the eyes of men of a certain quality. That was the only masculine touch about her, and for some reason those bright and brave eyes made all the delicacy of her features and her personality more distinct. As for McTee, he worshipped her. He wanted to fall on his knees and adore her. He wanted to take her in his arms and carry her away from the world that no eyes but his own might see her—that no voice, saving his, might address her—that no hand, saving his, might take both those small and soft brown hands of hers.

He closed his eyes, so fierce and quick was this rush of emotion. And he heard Donnelly, out of the dim distance, saying: "There wasn't no demons, Molly. There was only one hell-fire eating gent that come along and cleaned me up!"

"At your age? Oh, the horrible coward!"

"At my age?" he said, mimicking her wrath. "At my age I'll handle my guns with any of the youngsters. But this here stranger was a flash of lightning. There wasn't no getting away from him. Dog-gone me if he didn't shoot so fast, when he come through the door and got a glimpse of me swinging a shotgun his direction, that he fired and downed me before he seen that I was an old man."

"I suppose he said that?" cried the girl with a passionate scorn. "Tell me, Uncle Donnelly."

"Sure he said it. D'you think that I could've guessed it?"

"He lied," she cried, coming hastily to the side of the bunk where he lay. "He lied. He wanted to murder you. And only when he saw that his bullet had not. . . ."

"Don't you get to talking faster than you got a right to talk, honey."

"Where did the bullet go?"

"Right through the leg."

"Oh!"

"It ain't nothing at all. Just kind of ticklish at first."

"Where in the leg?"

"Well, above the knee."

"You poor dear. You poor old dear," moaned the girl.

"A great slug tearing through your flesh and smashing. . . . Oh!" She covered her face with her hands until a new thought made her look up. "And then he abandoned you!"

"He might be back," said Donnelly. "He just stepped out a little while ago."

"He's gone! He's gone, I say!"

"He left quite a lot of chuck before he went," said Donnelly. "Which I guess was pretty white of him."

"He left you food to quiet his conscience. But all the time he knew that you couldn't drag yourself out of bed to help yourself."

"He might not have knowed just how bad he'd laid me up."

"Didn't he bandage you?"

"Yes."

"Then he knew." Her scorn was a sword of fire.

"Molly, you dunno and I dunno what was in his head. He was riding like he had something mighty important to reach."

"The gallows! The gallows!" cried Molly. "That's what he's riding to reach. And, by the heavens, I'll have a posse of every decent man in the mountains hunting him down before. . . ."

"Hush up, Molly. You dunno what you're saying."

And McTee walked slowly around the little building, carrying his saddle with him. When he reached the door, he paused. The two were too much wrapped up in one another to pay any heed to him.

"I won't leave you," she was saying. "*I* won't leave you until you're back again on your feet."

"Why, Molly, you know that the boys will be home again tonight."

"The boys. . . ."

There was such a meaning in her pause that old Donnelly began to raise himself on his elbows.

"What d'you mean by looking at me like that, Molly?

What d'you mean when you speak of the boys like that?''

"I mean . . . oh, nothing as bad as you're thinking now. Only, they're both hurt."

"Both my boys?" whispered old Donnelly. "Both hurt? Heaven have mercy!"

The last three words were a great and stirring prayer.

"By a professional man-killer, Uncle Donnelly. So we'll simply thank heaven that they're still alive, and that they're going to get well. Both times that unspeakable devil missed them. . . ."

Was that the interpretation that the world put upon skill that had enabled him to strike down his enemies, and yet to spare their lives? He reflected bitterly that he might as well have killed every time he drew a gun.

"What's his name?" Donnelly was saying, grinding his teeth.

"Safety McTee."

"That fiend?"

"It's he. And. . . ."

Something like the falling of a shadow across her mind made her whirl around, and recognition and horror darkened in her eyes. She pointed at him as she shrank away.

"That's he! That's the man!"

Chapter Six

"A Bitter Accusation"

It was old Donnelly who put the common surmise into words.

"Then you come up here to put me out of the way. McTee, how the devil have I ever harmed you, or how have my boys ever harmed you?"

McTee could not answer. It was the girl who found appropriate words at once, recovering from her first fear. She confronted McTee with her color rising and her gray eyes bright.

"Can't you guess, Uncle Donnelly? He was hired by someone to murder you all. Someone wants your property. Someone . . . oh, I have it, that someone wants the mine!"

McTee, cold and sober, watched the face of Donnelly without letting his eyes change, and he saw the increasing shadow in the eyes of the old miner. Now the latter nodded.

"Maybe that's it. What d'you aim for now, McTee? Have

you come back to finish the thing that you couldn't finish before?''

"Donnelly," said McTee, "are you talking your own thoughts, or the thoughts this girl has put into your head?"

He saw Molly stiffen with rage and surprise. Indeed, he watched her with a sort of melancholy pleasure. For she was quite lost to him, and lost forever. And he might as well enjoy the pleasant picture that her anger made.

"I'm talking my own thoughts," said Donnelly. "And . . . is your name Safety McTee?"

"My name is McTee."

"But is it Safety McTee?"

The big man paused. He had never before been ashamed of that name. For it was famous in a thousand towns, a thousand camps. It was a trumpet that stirred men to fear. And it was also a passport that took him through all manner of dangerous passes. But he was ashamed now, and mightily.

"My name is McTee, and some folks call me Safety."

"Ah," said Donnelly after a short and terrible pause. "You're him, are you?"

With that he turned his head deliberately toward the girl as if, from that instant, he shut McTee entirely out of his thoughts.

Safety turned back to the outer air and sat down on a stone, with his square, hard chin resting upon the knuckles of one fist. There he thought the matter over. Something in his guilty soul told him that, if the old man had been there all alone, he would probably have ridden and even left him to his fate. But he could never leave the girl. Now that she had once taken hold of him, he could never escape. And he knew, also, that it could not be any passing fancy. He had been taken with girls many a time, flirted with them, danced with them, made small talk with them, dreamed of them pleasantly for a day or two, and then forgotten them completely. But Molly was not like the others. As he squinted up the mountainside, he could summon up her face into his

193

imagination as surely as though he had himself created it with his pencil. He knew every line of that face. He could sit there recalling her voice.

Suddenly she spoke behind him. "Will you tell me why you are staying here, Safety McTee? Are you screwing up your courage?"

"For what?" he asked as he turned to face her.

"To go back to the shack and finish the murder?"

He hesitated until the crimson had poured back out of his face and left him quite white.

"That," he said, "is mightily unfair. And you know it."

"You think that other people are going to think anything unfair that's been said about you, when they learn how you've hounded this poor family of three? And now you've shot down an old man of seventy. . . ."

"Don't," said McTee. "I swear that I didn't see his face. I was trying to get into the shack. . . ."

"Ah! You were breaking in! You were trying to burglarize his house, and, when he defended it, you. . . ." She could not continue the sentence. There was such rage in her eyes that he began to shrink in his own estimation until he was no more than a child in the presence of an inexorable teacher.

"I was hunting for the Donnelly house. I just tried to get in to make him tell me the way."

"You didn't know?"

"I didn't."

"And you shot him down . . . an old man . . . because he wouldn't answer?"

He made a pleading gesture as if for sympathy. "I was looking into a shadow," he said, "when I looked through the door. All that I saw was a man and the shine of the light on a shotgun's double barrel. There isn't any fooling with a shotgun. It squirts nothing but sure death at short range. So I pulled my revolver mighty quick and got in a shot just as he was whipping the muzzles of that gun around where they'd bear on me. I let him have it, but I fired low . . . on purpose. That was my way of making him helpless. D'you think that I would've shot that low, if I'd really wanted to kill him?''

"You're not the first man who's missed!''

He shook his head violently. "I'm different from the rest.''

"Ah?'' said she incredulously.

"But you understand,'' he explained, "that if I'd come here to . . . to *murder* him . . . I'd have finished him when he was dropped and down. . . .''

"I can well believe,'' said the girl, "that even the most hardened nerves would not be equal to the effort of butchering an old man already down.''

"But you think I shot him, then, to kill?''

"Mister McTee, you'll find a thousand men on the ranges who'll agree with me.''

Perspiration stood out upon the forehead of McTee.

"You're afraid of that, then?'' she asked, with a sort of impersonal curiosity, as if he were a biological specimen, and not a human being. "I thought that Safety McTee didn't know what the meaning of fear was?''

"I'm afraid of their guns,'' said McTee. "Guns can't do more'n knock the life out of a gent. But what folks say. . . .''

"Well?''

"What folks say can be a pile worse than anything that their guns say. I'd rather face two guns, any day, than one old woman that's started gossiping, or half of an old man.''

She stared at him in wonder. "You're most afraid,'' she said, "of losing your popularity?''

He flushed, again, at that. "I know,'' he said, "that they all hate me. But all the same, they all respect me. There isn't a one of 'em can say that I ever took an advantage. . . .''

"Until this very day,'' said the girl.

"You'll go talking this yarn about?''

"I've got to tell what I think.''

"You'll make 'em think that I'm just a murderer!''

"I'm sorry for that."

His face set savagely. For a single instant she was almost afraid that he was going to leap at her. But then the danger faded, and there remained only an appeal. There could be no doubt that he was in the most mortal anguish. For his reputation lay in her small hands, to destroy if she chose to destroy it.

"You've fought other people with guns. Why shouldn't you be fought in turn by having the truth told about you?"

"Listen to me," he said. "If you'll give me five minutes of time, I'll prove to you that I couldn't've missed him, standing anywhere near so close to him as I was standing there."

"How can you possibly prove that?"

"Like this, for one thing."

A gun appeared as if by magic in his hand. She watched the ease and precision with which it slipped over his finger-tips and the muzzle tipped up. Then that muzzle jerked sharply into the air. Thin smoke puffed straight out, and the explosion jarred against her ears.

He was pointing up the slope, and she followed the direction that he indicated with her eyes. She was in time to see a little shrub lean to one side and begin to roll down toward them.

"What's happened?" cried Molly.

It tumbled straight down to them. Then he raised it and showed it to her. The bullet he fired had clipped the narrow trunk squarely in two.

"You see?" he explained.

She touched the wood with awe and then looked curiously up to his face. There was not the slightest vainglory in his manner or in his expression. Instead, there was a deep anxiety. He was waiting for her verdict like a criminal for the decision of the judge.

"That was a good shot," she said. "Oh, nobody doubts

that you're a good shot. But, then, everybody misses now and then.''

''Not me. I never miss. With these here guns, and anything in pointblank range, I can't miss. It's just like my bullets were running down grooves that led straight to the things that I fire at.''

''Really?'' murmured the girl, and, absent-mindedly, she flicked a little pebble into the air.

It did not rise high, but it was still in the air when the left hand of McTee whipped out a gun that had hitherto been well concealed. The gun exploded. The bright little quartz pebble was jerked into nothingness out of mid-flight.

''Does that look like proof to you?'' he asked her.

''What's target practice?'' she said. ''There's a great difference between a target and a human being to shoot at.''

He groaned.

''Is there anything I can do to prove it to you?'' he said. ''Isn't there a thing that could show you that I didn't shoot him low by accident?''

''See that the boys are both safely back on their feet. Give that much back to them, and I'll begin to believe what you say.''

Chapter Seven

"Molly's Wild Ride"

She went back into the hut, and there she stood beside the bunk on which Donnelly lay stretched.

"What d'you make of him?" asked Donnelly.

"He's very strange."

"He's more than that. He's just damn' queer. Sometimes I been feeling myself almost up to liking him, Molly."

"So have ... he's got some good in him, perhaps," said Molly shrewdly. "But everyone has. And, in the meantime, I'm going to have him tried out. I'm going away from the shack a little bit. He'll think that I've gone to tell people that he tried to murder you. As a matter of fact, I'll be staying just on the other side of the hilltop. When he sees that I've gone, of course, he'll jump on his horse and ride as fast as he can. ..."

"I ain't so sure," said Donnelly. "I dunno that even

Safety McTee would go away, thinking that I was left here alone without no care of any sort.''

"Uncle Donnelly, that's a wild thing to say. He . . . he's a professional killer!''

"What was that shooting I been hearing?''

"He was showing me that he must have shot low on purpose at you because he's such a good shot that he couldn't have missed his real target at such a distance as he stood from you!''

"Eh?'' murmured Donnelly. "Well, he's taking this here to heart. Try that ride over the hill, and I'll bet you that two-year-old roan that you like so well. . . .''

"Bet me what?''

"I'll bet you that when you ride away as though you was going to take the news around the range, that Safety McTee ain't going to start away . . . he's going to come right back in here and start taking care of me.''

She waved her hand to him, almost gaily. She was flushed with excitement.

"Maybe you're hoping that. . . .''

But she ran out of the cabin, and, after a moment, he heard the clatter of the hoofs of her horse begin and sweep up the side of the hill. From the very top the noise beat down to him, for the top of that hill was a crown of solid rock. Then the noise was suddenly diminished to almost nothing. She was descending the farther slope.

Now was the trial for McTee. And the heart of the old miner leaped with triumph for an instant. There was no sound of McTee approaching to get his saddle. For a long minute there was not a sign of life from the big man. But, then, he must have sprung into action violently, as though he realized that each moment was precious to him if he wished to put distance between himself and the pursuit.

He ran in, having fully made up his mind to beat a retreat, caught up the heavy saddle, and dashed out again, whistling softly. That whistle brought to him the big bay, and the wounded man heard the saddle slapped upon the back of the horse. Then the straps groaned slightly as the cinches were drawn, a spur clinked, a foot struck into a heavy saddle, and there was a grunt from the horse as the bulk of the rider slumped suddenly onto his back.

The hoof beats began with a rush and with a rush they passed out of hearing to the west from the shack, straight down the gap, as a man would ride who wished to plunge at once into the intricate mazes of the upper mountains, where a thousand little valleys and ravines sliced across one another. But even here the fugitive would not be safe. For the law would prove too many in numbers, too steady in arm for him to escape from it. All the great ones went down before it. Donnelly reviewed them one by one, the famous outlaws and the desperadoes whose names had filled the imagination of the youth of the country at one time or another, but whose wrists eventually filled the steel circles of a pair of handcuffs. And all of those winding and difficult roads in the mountains through which it seemed so impossible to pursue a man were eventually traps in which the refugees were hunted down. It would be so with Safety. But how terrible would his record be before he was captured?

Donnelly saw the fall, the grave, the talk after the death of McTee, and then he roused himself from a sigh to hear the beat of hoofs again. It was the slow and steady beat of a horse coming at a trot. Certainly it could not be Molly returning. She would come like a whirlwind in triumph, laughing and shouting, for that was Molly's way.

The hoof beats ended beside his door. And in the doorway stood the big form of Safety McTee.

"What's wrong?" said Donnelly. "Don't you know that the girl has gone, McTee? Don't you know that she's going to send a posse back here? If you want to save yourself, ride as fast as the devil."

But McTee shook his head. "I guess here's where I stay,"

he said. "She'll most likely send back the boys to hunt me. But in case she didn't...."

"Well?" said Donnelly.

"What would become of you, Donnelly?"

"I'll be all right."

"You've got a fever rising. You'll be all right, if you get care, and that's the only way you *will* be all right."

"You talk like a fool, McTee! Why, if they come back and find you here...."

"They won't find me, if they come. I'll be off on old Bones. Now shut up your talking and lemme hear no more language. You might be needing your strength."

The girl had been watching from the top of the hill—had seen McTee ride away from the shack. She had not waited to watch him out of sight, for, if she had, she would have seen him turn and start back again. Instead, she turned the head of her horse in another direction and galloped away.

She did not let her horse come to a walk during the entire ride, but pressed him relentlessly forward until she reached a small town dropped like a wedge into the crevice between two mountains. A torrent ran through the same pass, and it crowded the town to one side, but what there was of the town had an air of reckless defiance. There was no particular reason why it should exist in this place. It had grown up haphazard, and it showed its fortune in its face, so to speak. Its population had risen to fifteen hundred, once, before there was a mining rush for a neighboring region. And still the outer rind of that existence showed where the limits of the little place had bulged out on either side up and down the ravine. But these shacks were long since deserted, and now the sky and the weather looked through them whenever they chose, although in the core of the town there was still an inhabited kernel, and it was toward this that the girl sent her horse flying.

The first man she met was a small rancher from the Black Hills beyond the eastern range, but, though she knew him well, and though he greeted her with a shout and a wave of his hat when he saw her in the distance, yet she tickled her mare with the spur and flashed past him without a turn of the head or a flash of the eye.

She knew, without looking around, that he was following. His was one of the ranches which was in her basket. In that basket lay some of the choicest ranches along the range. And there were great forests and rich mines in the same carryall. For in her hand she held the hearts of the owners, and whatever they had they would give into her keeping.

She passed another of her adherents as she flew along the one long street. And he, also, turned, uncalled, and followed her at a tremendous gallop. She plunged past the blacksmith shop. She flew on to the hotel and general merchandise store. There she flung herself from her horse just as Al Demming and Lefty came rushing up behind.

There is a certain rhythm about the flying hoofs of a horse that will rouse the hearts of men like the peal of an alarm bell or the cry of fire. For who can say that the gallop of a horse bearing an angry man is the same as the gallop of a horse bearing a fugitive?

Before Molly drew rein, half a dozen loungers had extricated themselves from the delicious reveries in which they were lost in the evening of the day. They stood up and glared at her, anticipating news that would force them to throw away silken ease and become men of action for the nonce.

They received the news at once. She jumped up to the railing of the hotel and balanced herself there with her hair blowing and her eyes shining and her sweet, high voice thrilling through the door and up the corridor of the hotel. It passed up and down the street, also, and instantly men began to rush out.

Women came also, but more slowly. So that the inner core of the crowd that jammed itself around Molly was entirely composed of men. Then she told them what had happened in the mountains. She told them that the man who had struck down the two Donnelly boys—for the news of that had already come to the town—had followed along their back trail until he reached the father of the boys and had struck him down as well! She did not need to be eloquent upon that subject. The mere mention of the facts was enough to infuriate them. Apparently there were men here who had had experience of the prowess of McTee, and who had already spent time talking to one another about their experiences. Their shout of rage was like the sudden and discordant blast of a dozen trumpets. Then they plunged for their horses.

And Molly, still standing on the rail and looking down the street, saw man after man dart out from his yard, followed by a rolling, boiling cloud of white dust that jerked to the side and coiled away down the street. A dozen, twenty men started in that fashion. There was no sheriff to represent the restraining hand of the law. What would happen when that irresistible force struck the immovable object—Safety McTee?

Chapter Eight

"Molly's Ride"

To Molly it was like the riding forth of knights in a just war. Every yard of the way from the Donnelly shack to the town her anger against McTee had been growing. To her, the Donnelly family was nearer and dearer than blood relations in many ways. For her father had been under deep and lasting obligations to the rough miner in his youth. It was Donnelly who had stood by him in danger and in work. Donnelly who had taught him all he knew of the mining game. It was Donnelly, again, who had advised him to break away from the mines and sink the small fortune that he had made in hunting gold in the safer venture of cattle raising. The fortune that he could not make for himself, he had made for the father of Molly Carson. But the bond between the two families was far, far deeper and stronger than any money obligation. And Molly had grown up to look upon the Donnelly boys as allies and comrades and upon their father as something more than any uncle could be.

And here was the whole family within an ace of being wiped out by a single destroyer. She had shuddered and gasped while the horse galloped on. And now she watched with joy while the avengers started out in such haste along the trail.

It was not until the last man had ridden from the town that she began to remember that, after all, neither her uncle nor his two sons had been actually slain by the gunfighter. But whatever her considerations were now, they must be too late, for she had launched a bolt of destruction that she could not call back.

In the shack of Donnelly, the evening wore into darkness, and McTee built up the fire, for the wind was turning sharp and raw of edge. He built up the fire until the chimney roared and trembled with the rushing of the draft. Then he cooked supper with equal speed and deftness. He fried bread, he made such coffee as is more often dreamed of than tasted, and he composed a stew of a thousand fragments that, united, formed a delightfully harmonious whole.

Before that meal was over they were the happiest of companions. The wound in Donnelly's leg was in very good shape. And his pleasure in the conversation of his guest was quite sufficient to drown the pain of the hurt. For the deep and pleasant voice of McTee was telling stories that ranged from the Pampas to the Yukon. Moreover, he was not talking about himself, but always of a friend, or a chance acquaintance, and some wild adventure.

Their supper was ended. Their pipes were filled, smoked out, and filled again. And then they heard the coming of the horses.

The ears of Donnelly had been tuned sharp by the many years of lonely living and lonely hunting. But the ears of

McTee had caught the sound long before the older man heard and understood. He leaped up in the middle of a sentence and stood motionless in the center of the floor.

"What is it?" asked Donnelly.

"They've come for me."

"How . . . good heavens, boy, what're you going to do?"

"There are about twenty of 'em," said McTee thoughtfully.

The first noises of the beating hoofs came down to Donnelly. "They'll massacre you, son. Jump into your saddle and run for it!"

McTee remained standing, but, instead of rushing for the door, he continued to fill his pipe.

"You ain't gone crazy, McTee?"

"I dunno but what I have."

"Why are you stayin' here?"

"I haven't got the heart to run away."

"How come? What you mean?"

"If I run away, I never see her again, Donnelly."

"See who?" asked Donnelly sharply.

"Besides," said McTee without answering the last query, "if I run for it now, I can never show my face to the law again. And it's pretty hard to get along living all by yourself."

"You think so? I thought you were always by yourself?"

"Not me. I used to figure that I was as wild as a wild goose. But I'm not. Not by a damn' sight, partner. I used to think that I was cut out to stand off the rest of the world while I went along the way I picked out for myself."

He rubbed his hard knuckles across his chin, and the miner, grinding down the cinder in his pipe bowl, studied his companion with a sort of melancholy interest.

"You got mighty little time left," he declared, as the rumbling of the hoofs increased perceptibly so that it became possible to pick out the rattling of the individual horses.

"I've got time enough," said the gunfighter as steadily as

before, "to make up my mind to stay right where I am. And here I stay till they come for me."

There came a new gleam in the eye of the old miner.

"You're going to fight it out with 'em right here?" he said. "You're going to let 'em close in on you and then show 'em your teeth?"

McTee flushed. In a wave, all the blood of his body seemed to rush to his face, and in a wave it left him pale. He smiled down at the wounded man and showed a white and even row of teeth—a mirthless smile.

"I'll stay without fighting," he said. "I'm tired of fighting. I'm going to try what waiting things out will do for me."

"McTee, would you try reason on wolves?"

"Well?"

"A lynching mob is worse to argue with than wolves."

He stopped, his voice breaking sharply away, for the swift volleying of the hoofs now began to drown their thoughts. It was too late to flee. All that they could do was to stand fast and watch whatever was to take place.

"But if they'll listen," cried Donnelly heartily, "I'll sure send 'em away ashamed that they ever come up here for you. You can lay to that, my boy. I ain't going to talk up ag'in' you, either soft or loud."

McTee did not seem to hear. He had seated himself again and was contemplating the farther wall of the room with a sort of sad content.

"And yet," he said, "I wonder if she'd understand when it was over and done with?"

Donnelly stared at him with popping eyes. He could not understand such talk. What woman could McTee refer to, when it was known to every man that he had no care for the gentler sex? But Donnelly had been with other men just before their deaths, and many and many a time he had seen them act strangely, heard them talk strange words, as though the shadow of their approaching fate had fallen before their feet and already involved their minds. Perhaps the same madness had fallen upon McTee. Perhaps in another moment or so the strong body would be chained up in motionlessness forever, and the active mind would be sleeping in a sleep that could not be broken.

Before those solemn thoughts had flowered, the storm of men struck the house with an effect very like the breaking of a storm of wind and rain. The shoulder of a stumbling horse struck the shack and made the crazy building shake and shudder throughout, while at the same time a storm of noises beat around them, then the neigh of a fleeing horse, far-off, like the yell of the wind as it leaps down a great valley.

There was an explanation of that sound. A voice cried: "Get that big hoss. That's McTee's hoss. And if we got the hoss, McTee will have the half of his teeth drawed. It's the hoss that's kept him a free man all these here years. But if the hoss is here, the man will be here. Scatter around the shack, boys!"

"Who is that?" murmured McTee, his voice raised just high enough to reach the ear of his companion but not to penetrate the flimsy wall.

"That's McKim."

"From Dunning River?"

"That same."

"He's a hard man, they say."

"He's harder than hard. He's a devil. He likes nothing but trouble. That's the style of McKim."

"Listen to him run this crowd."

For the voice of McKim was constantly taking the lead and giving the directions to the others.

"Lemme do the talking," he said now. "The rest of you just keep quiet for a while so's one gent can be heard giving instructions. If anybody wants to give them instructions better than me, let him turn loose!"

No one spoke, and McKim continued loudly. "Keep scattered around the house. Get a bunch on each corner. If anything shows, don't do no talking. Start shooting. After it drops, we'll ask the questions later on.''

There was a deep-throated murmur of assent. And Donnelly glanced sharply across at McTee. Yet he saw that the big man was not yet weakening. In fact, he merely shrugged his shoulders and smiled.

"They're all with McKim," said McTee softly. "They've ridden so far and so hard to get me that now they want me mighty bad."

"Maybe there's a brother of some of your dead men in that crowd," said the old miner.

"Maybe there is," said McTee, and still his color did not change.

"Hello!" called the voice of McKim. "Are you there, Donnelly?"

The raised hand of McTee checked the response of the miner.

"By heavens!" cried McKim on the outside. "He's murdered the old man, and now he's sitting in there as quiet as you please. You can smell the supper that the hound cooked out of Donnelly's chuck."

"McTee!" roared a dozen voices.

There was no answer.

"Let's rush the shack!"

"Me first and through the door," answered McKim, who was not lacking in courage.

His heavy knock fell against the door. Then he cast it open and stepped in. Behind him thronged a dozen faces.

Chapter Nine

"Beneath the Spruce"

The picture that they saw shocked them to a pause. There lay the presumed victim snugly in his bed with a well-browned corncob between his teeth, and his eyes dull with the enjoyment of the tobacco. And yonder sat the presumed murderer, likewise smoking. His eyes, however, were not dull. His features were as immobile as rock, but his eyes were gleaming and glancing like polished metal, and, wherever a ray from them fell, that man winced on whom the light touched.

The whole body of the crowd gave back a little before the pair they confronted. They seemed actually dismayed to find Donnelly alive and apparently very well.

"Well, boys," said Donnelly, "you seem to have got all het up about something. What's wrong? What's the party headed for?"

Instead of reply with words, they glowered down at him.

210

"He's been bought up by McTee," said McKim suddenly.

"That's what it is," roared another.

The man pushed himself out from the others, shaking himself free as a dog shakes away the water. He confronted McTee.

"D'you know me, McTee?"

"I dunno that I do. Who are you?"

"I'm Bill Salmon."

"Dunno that I place that name."

"Ever know Harry Salmon?"

"Didn't I hear that something happened to Harry down at Tonopah . . . ?"

"You skunk!" Salmon snarlingly replied. "Don't we all know that you was the one that plugged him and then ran for it like a yaller cur?"

His gun was half drawn as he spoke. And there were other guns in the background which were not only drawn but leveled. The least gesture of McTee would bring a shower of lead upon him. But the only gesture he made was to lower his forefinger and press the coal of his pipe deeper into the tobacco.

"You're starting in taking water," offered Bill Salmon sneeringly. "That's your speed when you get in a corner, eh?"

"That's my speed," said McTee, "when a rat comes to bother me. I don't waste no powder and lead on him. I wait till I can catch the rat in a trap."

Salmon blinked. Then he saw that he had been flagrantly insulted before all of these spectators, and he tore out the gun from the holster. But still McTee did not stir. Even when the revolver was leveled against him, his eyes held unwaveringly upon the face of Salmon.

"Yes, that's it," he repeated. "A rat! Damned if you don't look like a cornered rat to me, now!"

The revolver jerked up in the hand of Billy Salmon, but it did not explode. He cursed with a sort of feeble futility and moved away. The others from the rear of the crowd pressed forward, now, around McTee. The ice had been broken. And they were anxious to get their hands upon their victim. Yet McTee did not move, did not speak.

To Donnelly such nerve was so wonderful, knowing that every man in that crowd asked nothing better than a chance to become famous by sinking a bullet in the body of the gunfighter, that he could not speak before this point. Then he talked up in haste.

"Boys, what's got you here?"

"What does it look like?" snapped out one to him.

"Like you mean trouble for somebody. Who is it . . . and why is it?"

"There's a murderer that's done his last killing."

"You mean McTee, I guess, because he's a fighter?"

"We mean him!"

"Lads, who did he ever drop that didn't have more than a fair show against him?"

There was no answer. But, instead of being appeased by this argument, the crowd seemed more and more angered, because it was being slightly opposed. It made its anger seen.

"Tell me one thing . . . what put you in bed, Donnelly?"

"I was cleaning a revolver, and the damned thing went off and sent a slug through my leg."

There was a groan of disbelief.

"It might've turned out serious," said the miner, "if McTee hadn't happened along just then and dressed that hole in my leg. He done a good job, and then he settled down to take care of me and make me comfortable."

"D'you know what he done to your boys?"

"I know what he done. He and me are both sorry. But they'll be wiser boys when they can walk again."

"The old hound has been bought off so's he denies his own boys!"

"I heard you say that, Larry Peters. And damn me if you could speak it so easy if I was on me feet again!"

Someone else picked up the ugly and infectious thought.

"McTee has handed Donnelly some money. They've worked it out between 'em to keep quiet about all this. But we ain't rode all this way to be stopped without doing nothing. Let's get some action started here!"

Not that one man said all of these things, but they were contributed from several quarters, and made up a dull and deep muttering—the indistinguishable voice of a mob when it means mischief.

"What'll we do first?" said McKim hastily, as though afraid that the credit for leading this gang might pass out from his hands.

"The first thing is to find out if he's guilty."

"Of what?"

"Of murder."

"What murder has he done here?"

"It ain't the murder that he's done here, but it's the murders that he's done in other places," said McKim. "He's the sort of a killer that plays the game safe, and that nobody never lays a hand on. Because he works behind a fence. He's got the law between him and trouble all of the time. Ain't that right?"

There was an instant assent.

"Of course, it's right."

"Then what we got to do is to get rid of him . . . if he's done what he hadn't ought to've done."

There was a general nodding of heads. Slowly the crowd was fumbling its way toward its purpose.

"McTee, stand right out here where we can have a look at you!"

"I've been looking for a judge or a sheriff or something in this here crowd," he said. Then he yawned in their faces. "But I don't see anybody that represents the law," he said, "and I dunno that I see anybody that I feel like listening to."

It was such insane insolence in the face of such a danger

213

that a muttering which was almost a groan came from the other men in the room. And Donnelly reared himself high on his elbows with a cry.

"McTee," he said, "what's happened to your brains?"

"I can't be bothered with these," said McTee. "I've been working with men, most of my life, and, when such a gang of coyotes as these here come flocking around yapping at me, it sort of makes me sick, damned if it don't. I'm through with the fight, old son. Let 'em take me, if they want me. There isn't no use lifting a hand ag'in' a dozen men."

"Take him," said one from the rear of the group, and being in the rear, he did not feel the fear that kept the more forward members back from the seated outlaw. The wave of motion that he started now rolled straight forward and engulfed McTee at once. And the minute the posse came in contact with him, it began to snarl like a pack of dogs around a wolf.

He was jerked to his feet, and his hands bound behind him in a trice. He was led to the door of the cabin and through it.

"We need the outside air to handle McTee in," someone said, and that idea seemed so natural, it seemed so impossible to deal with one of his magnitude in the narrow confines of that shack, that there was not the slightest argument. They brought him into a loose circle of young fir trees near the cabin. In the center of the circle there was a great spruce. Over one of the lower branches they threw a rope and led McTee beneath the tree. Yet they hesitated. Such a situation as this called for momentous words from someone of those present. And McTee refused to speak to them. When he was asked if he repented his life of violence, he replied with a sneer. When he was asked if he had any last requests, he told them simply that he had never trusted business during his life to dogs, and that he would hate to have his words whined about by hounds.

Such messages as these were hardly the sort that the posse could take back and repeat with any sweet savor through the cattle ranges.

"Let's have a little light on this here!" said someone.

He kindled some bark, as he spoke, and held a wisp of it in a close huddle of the branches of one of the firs. At once the flames began. There was a noisy sputtering and crackling of the needles. Then a yellow arm of flame leaped up, put out a hand for an upper branch, failed to grasp it securely, sank away, tried again, and finally caught a finger hold on the bough above. An instant more and the whole side of the tree was in flames, bodies of fire shooting into the air high above their heads.

"You damn' fool, Stevens," called McKim. "What if the forest ranger should come along and see us lighting trees for torches? He'd slam the whole lot of us in prison. Or suppose that some of the sparks was to blow over and start a forest fire going. . . ."

"You've talked enough, McKim," said the other savagely. "Damn all that sort of lingo. What I want is action, and here's a light for us to see what we're doing!"

The others agreed. Even the action of McKim lasted hardly more than an instant. For there was the fire, rising and whirling. With a savage shout, they fastened the noose around McTee's neck.

Then came that voice out of the outer blackness that all of them were to remember, each to his dying day. "In the name of heaven, don't do that murder!"

They started and turned to see who had come upon them. And what they saw was Donnelly. For the old man had dragged himself, in spite of his wounded leg, out of the house and across the rough ground, and now he lay in agony on the edge of the clearing, still straining to pull himself nearer, though his strength would no longer serve to bring him forward. And at the sight of the man who had been shot down by McTee, lying there, pleading for the life of his oppressor, a groan broke simultaneously from the throats of the men of the posse.

Chapter Ten

"Donnelly Speaks Again"

Clouds in the central sky were broken apart, and through
them the moon looked down suddenly as though searching
the earth for a hidden guilt. The leaping fires from the burning tree died away as the wind died. And all at once there
was a cessation of noise. No one spoke. The shadows swept
across the open space, from side to side. The flames in the
tree were falling to nothing as the foliage from the outer
branches was consumed. The pitchy needles had given forth
one great flare. But the body of the tree had been barely
ignited. Its branches and its trunk were fringed with flick-
ering lines of flame, but the light it sent forth was less strong
than the pale moonshine that was flooding down more and
more strongly upon the mountains.

And, by that light, the posse grew uneasy. Man looked to
man, but in the face of the other he found the same uneasy

gloom that he already felt in his own heart. And still they were undetermined.

Then the voice of old Donnelly came from the shadows: "But after you've murdered him, the end ain't yet. The end ain't with the killing of McTee," cried Donnelly. "I know your faces. I've seen you all. And, by heaven, I ain't going to forget. The sheriff has got to know. I'll tell him that you was up here, McKim!"

The swelling import of McKim seemed to shrink by one half.

"And I've knowed your face, Al Peters. And I seen you, McCutcheon. And you, Parkins. And you, LeRoy!

"The sheriff will have you, one by one. Unless you want to leave your home and your wife and your kids, Melloy, and ride for it into the hills . . . and you the same, Saunders, and you, Jackson. . . ."

The leveled forefinger which checked them off had the effect of a revolver discharged at each gesture. They gave back. Each name he spoke blasted another man from the circle of those hard riders. They shrank away. The tie that had bound them together was broken.

"I'm through," said the oldest of the party suddenly. "Damned if I don't wish that I'd never come. It was your fool talk, McKim, that started this!"

McKim, however, was too frightened to answer. He was torn between several chilly fears. On the one hand, that place in which they all stood was becoming more and more ghostly in spite of the presence of so many men. And, again, McTee might be writing down names and faces in his memory. When he was free once more, it would be to take the trail of those who had attacked him, and first of all he would take the trail of the ringleader, McKim. To be sure, there was also the sheriff to dread, but where was there a sheriff for an instant comparable with the terror-breathing figure of McTee? No, better, far better to risk the full anger of the sheriff, rather than take a chance on McTee.

He jerked his revolver from its holster and poised it. He was both fast and sure with a Colt. At such a distance he was certain that he could not miss such a target.

"That's murder," someone was shouting, and damned him.

It filled the cup of McKim. He turned, tore himself from the others, and fled.

That was only the beginning of fear, however. Panic is the most contagious of diseases. It pours out like water and sweeps through every brain. So it swept, now, through the minds of the good men of the posse. Not a man there but was brave. But, taken altogether, they made up a mob, and a mob has the brain and the heart of a brute. Instantly they were blind with fear. They ran for their horses and spurred away over the hills and through the pass back to the town as though there were furies behind them, and the faster they fled, the more vivid became the picture in their imaginations of McTee rushing for his horse and flying in the pursuit. Every instant, from behind them, the night gave up the dreadful shadow of his approaching form. And, without a word spoken, they plunged back to the town, whirled apart, and there made what preparations they could to meet the gunfighter when he should come.

McTee seemed to recover the full possession of his senses in a trice. "I can see that there isn't any call for a hurry," he said to Donnelly. "The thing to do is to go slow and get 'em, one by one."

"McTee! McTee! There was twelve of them, if there was one. Would you do twelve killings?"

"Wouldn't I?" said McTee. "Ah, man, d'you think that I can sleep easy so long as I know that there's one of them skunks living and talking about how they caught McTee?"

"You can lay to it, there ain't going to be no talking done. They was a scared lot when they left these parts."

"They're scared now, but they'll get over it. I know the way talk leaks out and runs."

219

"But you're wrong, McTee. You're wrong! There ain't a man of 'em that ain't ashamed of what he's done up here tonight."

"Ashamed?" groaned McTee. "D'you think I care for their shame? What I want to know is . . . when are they going to bleed for what they've done? That's what I want to know!"

Donnelly shook his head. "If it's going to be that way, then I'm sorry that I. . . ." He paused.

"You're sorry you saved me, old captain? But I'll make you glad before you're through with me, Donnelly."

McTee had already removed the noose from around his neck, and now he picked up the old miner as if the latter had been a child, and carried him back to the shack. There he made the other comfortable. He built up the fire. He made some coffee. But he himself touched nothing. And neither of them spoke for some time, until Donnelly could stop panting from his exertion.

"But," groaned Donnelly, "there was a dozen of 'em. What shame can that be to you?"

"That I didn't die fighting 'em! That I had to wait for a poor old cripple to come out and beg me from them . . . my heavens, I'm going to go plumb batty just thinking about it! But what kept me there like a fool while they closed in on me? What kept me from grabbing my gun and. . . ."

"Common sense. You knew that it would have been the same as suicide, McTee."

"Common sense? You dunno me," said McTee. "No, it was because she. . . ."

"Because what? Is there a woman mixed up somewhere in this here mess?"

But McTee returned no answer—that is, he returned no answer in words. Instead, he walked to the wall and took from it his gun belt and gun. He buckled these about him. He took down his sombrero from another peg and placed it upon his head. And Donnelly watched with a frown which grew blacker and blacker.

"Well," he said at length, "what is it?"

"I'm going to get me a man," said McTee. "I'm going to get me a man before the noon of tomorrow."

"How?" said Donnelly. "D'you think that you can capture houses full of armed men?"

"McKim isn't going to stay inside of any house," said McTee. "What he wants right now is cover, but, when the morning comes, he'll figure that a hundred eyes are watching for him. He'll begin to hanker for miles and more miles between him and me. So he'll run out to his barn and spur away north and north. . . ."

McTee stretched out his long arms with a sigh of joyous anticipation.

"And when he gets into the throat of the gap, when he gets into the heart of the hollow on the other side of the town, I'll be waiting for him there. I'll be waiting for him there!"

Donnelly stared for one instant into the face of the gunfighter. Then he dropped his chin on his chest and said not a word. For he knew that words were worse than useless.

Chapter Eleven

"Getting His Men"

It happened as though McTee had foreknowledge of what was to be. When McKim, that next morning, spurred up the ravine from the town, with his apprehensive glances turned behind him, he was snaked out of the saddle by a clean cast with a lariat. The rope girdled him beneath the pits of his arms, plucked him forth, and sat him down in the roadway some distance back. Before he had drawn a second breath, he was bound, hand and foot, and found himself extended prone in the dust of that trail.

A wisp of that same dust was blowing up and making a mist before the face of McTee, who towered above his victim. McKim said nothing. There was nothing to be said. And, as a matter of fact, he was not able to speak his mind for the next three days. During that time he lay in a bed in the town, raving in a delirium from which his poor mother feared that he would never recover.

For at noon of that unhappy day a horse plunged into the village with a rider bound to his back. When they stopped the horse and removed the rider, they found that it was no other than McKim, but McKim sadly altered from his gay self. He was naked to the waist. Upon his back a quirt had been used with such strength and skill that the skin either puffed into great wales or else was sliced through.

On the third day he recovered enough to tell them that it had been the terrible McTee who had struck him down. But he could have spared that information. It was known already. For Saunders, the day following the accident to McKim, was surprised while he was jogging home from a country dance. The story Saunders told was that, as the cart passed beneath the overhanging branch of a tree, the monster body of McTee had dropped on him, bound him, and then he had been beaten even more terribly than McKim.

That was the tale as Saunders put it. But little Jerry Munson happened to be sneaking home from a moonlight swim in the pool, and it was Jerry who gave the first insight into the methods of the outlaw as they really were.

"I seen the cart coming and figured that it might be Dad, coming back from Uncle Jeff's," said Jerry. "So I ducked into the brush and waited for the cart to go by. It didn't get far. About twenty steps past me something dropped out of the tree and sprawled Saunders out of the seat and into the road. Then I seen it was McTee, by his size and the way he was talking, and I was too scared to run away. I thought he'd murder me if he seen me.

"He was telling Saunders that Saunders was a skunk. But he was offering Saunders free hands and a gun if Saunders would get up and fight him, face to face, with an even chance to draw. But Saunders wouldn't say nothing. He just shook his head. So finally McTee said that he would get something worse than a bullet. He told him to stand up and defend himself.

"Saunders, when he seen that he was free and that McTee

223

wasn't holding a gun on him, give a yell like he couldn't believe what he seen. Then he jumps at McTee, hitting out with both hands. But McTee pulls a little back from him. He was backing up with a bad-looking smile on his face, like he was ready to kill Saunders but hadn't just decided where to put his hands first. Then he jumped in and just slid right through the punches of Saunders. There wasn't no fight to it, to speak of, after that.

"He hit Saunders, and Saunders went down. He got up and went down again.

" 'Damn you,' says Saunders, 'you ain't human!' and he jumps up and starts to run. But McTee got him before he'd gone two steps. Then he tied him up and whipped him on his bare back with a quirt. Pretty soon Saunders begin to yell and holler for help, till it turned my blood cold. Then he begun to groan. Finally he didn't make no sound, and there was nothing but the crackling of the lashes ag'in' his skin. Then McTee cut the ropes off'n him, throwed him in the cart, and yelled at the hoss.

"And he hollered after Saunders . . . 'Tell the rest of the swine that hounded me that I'm going to stay on their trail until I get 'em all just the same way that I got McKim and you. If any of them have got the guts to fight, I'll finish their business for 'em. If they're all yaller like you and McKim, they'll get what you and McKim have got!' "

When the story that Jerry had to tell arrived in the town, there were two meetings. On the one hand, the ten men remaining of the twelve who had attacked McTee gathered together and took council as to how they could avert these great impending evils. They ended by swearing that they must and should live close together, one prepared to fight for all the others, until they were rid of the common peril. The other assemblage consisted of the sheriff, two of his most trusted deputies, and some of the older men, including several of the fathers of the twelve.

What the fathers wanted was the scalp of McTee. What the sheriff wanted was a little patience.

"For," he said, "your folks started taking the law into their own hands. And damned if it don't do me good to see a mob getting hunted by the gent they mobbed."

So the matter rested there. The indignant fathers vowed that the sheriff was serving his last term of office. The sheriff smiled and declared that McTee, at least, would vote for him. But a day later the sheriff's mind changed. The matter had become serious in a new and important way.

For McTee had met one of the twelve, at last, whose dread of the gun of McTee was less than his dread of a personal shame. He dared to take the chance that was offered to him after he had been surprised and captured just like the other two. And, as a result, Sam Wilson dropped onto the dead brown grass with a bullet through his body.

McTee bandaged the wound and bore the body to a neighboring house. But there it lay for three days, and the two doctors who fought for Sammy's life did not know whether he would live or die.

Finally it was seen that he was to live. But that was no fault of McTee's. He had shot to kill. Only a little steel-lined wallet had made the bullet swerve from the straight line to the heart of Sammy. The sheriff could not avoid that proof. He did not try. The evening of Sammy's hurt he announced with a sigh that he was about to make a little more history for the range. He gathered more deputies, swore them in, and made ready to start.

But he started on the trail of McTee in a strange fashion. First of all, he went to the house of Molly's father at the edge of the town, and there he found Molly at home.

"Molly," he said at once, "who was the man that come to call on you along after dark last night?"

Molly looked at him coldly between the eyes. "I don't know what you're talking about, Sheriff," she said. "But I know that you're not trying to insult me."

The sheriff grinned. "Once upon a time I used to insult my wife the same way, whispering to her outside her window after dark. Nope, I don't mean no insult, Molly. But the other night it sort of seemed to me that I seen a man outside your window."

"Have you been spying?" snapped out Molly.

"Sure I ain't. I was just passing by."

Molly led him to the window.

"Nobody just passing by down the alley can see my window. That there hedge shuts off their view."

The sheriff was forced to blush. "I'd change places with you, if I could, Molly," he said. "Damned if I ain't an old blunderer. The trouble is while you'd make a mighty smart sheriff, I'd make a mighty wrinkled Molly. But are we still going to be friends?"

"I hope so," said Molly doubtfully. "But why have you been watching me?"

"Because I thought that it was Safety McTee that was calling on you."

As he spoke, he sharpened his scrutiny so that she felt his prying curiosity as effectively as a reaching hand. Yet the direct and easy fashion in which she met his eye would have seemed proof enough that she was innocent of the charge.

"Sheriff," she said, "it's hard to believe that I'm hearing you straight. You ask me if I been having that murderer come to call on me?"

"Well," said the sheriff, "I wouldn't exactly call him a murderer."

"You wouldn't?" said the girl indifferently. "Then you're the first I've met that has another opinion."

"Safety McTee is a gent that was born to take chances with guns just the way other gents are born to take chances with cards or hosses, y'understand?"

"But he plans them out, cold-blooded."

"He shoots to knock his men down, not to kill 'em. . . ."

226

"Ah, but that's only because he has practiced all his life, and he knows that he can't help but win."

"There's a lot of others around these parts that have practiced with guns all of their lives, and I'll tell you that anybody that invites a hundred-percent cowpuncher to pull guns with him is tapping at the door of death."

The sheriff had waxed actually poetic, but he tempered this elevated language with a broad grin.

"You've done a lot of tapping, then," said the girl.

"We're talking about McTee," said the sheriff.

"I'm tired of talking about him," said the girl.

The sheriff nodded. "Well," he said, "I'm mighty glad to hear that."

"Why?"

"Because I was worrying. I thought that, if you was a little fond of this McTee, you'd be sort of sorry to hear the news."

She riveted her eyes on his face.

"Yes?" she inquired faintly.

"McTee was run down and killed this morning," said the sheriff.

And, behold, Molly slumped suddenly to her knees.

Chapter Twelve

"Molly Plays a Part"

The sheriff picked her up. "I'm a dog, but this here thing had to be done, Molly!"

"It isn't true?" she begged.

"It ain't true, Molly. Safety McTee is as safe this minute as he ever was in his life, so far as I know."

She cast an impatient glance upward.

"I'm mighty ashamed that I used such a low-down trick on you about him," said the sheriff.

"I don't care . . . all I care about is that it wasn't true. You swear to that?"

"On my word of honor." He added, after he had stood for a moment scanning her face in which the color was stealing gradually back: "Molly, it was only a guess that I made. But, thank heaven, that guess was right."

"You'll tell folks about it, I know," said Molly. "What do I care for that?"

She made a great gesture of scorn. "If he should ever want to come to me, he'd come in spite of a thousand sheriffs!"

"Aye," said the sheriff, "that'll do to think right now. But later on, you'll begin to change your mind around a bit, maybe. You'll remember that a thousand men are a thousand men, and that one man is only one man."

She nodded sullenly. "If I tell you the truth, will you try to believe me?" she said.

"I'll try, Molly."

"Last night was the first night that ever he came to see me. He whispered outside the window for two minutes, and then he was gone again . . . oh, the wild, wild man to come into such a danger for the sake of saying half a dozen words. . . ."

But Molly was smiling divinely as she remembered those words.

"I'm mighty sorry," said the sheriff. "But when he comes back tonight, there'll be a reception committee waiting for him."

She cried out sharply, so that the nerves of the sheriff jumped.

"No, no! That would be . . . horrible murder!"

"It would be an easy way to capture him, Molly!"

"He'd fight till he'd killed twenty, even if they beat him down at last."

"He was took before," reminded the sheriff.

"It was because he had seen me that day. He thought that I . . . that I . . . anyways, he didn't care what happened to him that day. But now . . . but now he does care . . . and he'd be a tiger!"

There seemed to be no argument.

The sheriff began to walk up and down. Finally he started nodding, as though he were agreeing violently with a conclusion that he had proposed to himself.

"We got to do one of two things," said the sheriff. "We

got to get McTee into a prison, or else off this here range. Either way is a good way.''

She nodded, watching him mutely.

"But who could get him off?'' said the sheriff. "Who could get within talking distance of him without having him begin some of his hell raising?'' He answered himself suddenly: "You could, Molly! And you're the one to go to him!''

"If I could find him. But where shall I find him?''

"Up to Donnelly's house.''

"Do you think he'll be coming there?''

"Didn't he tell you he was there most of the time?''

"I . . . we . . . he didn't happen to mention it,'' said Molly.

"Well, he's there. How would old Donnelly get along without McTee to take care of him? When the boys decided to hunt down McTee. . . .''

"The cowards!'' put in Molly.

"They forgot that they were taking away Donnelly's nurse and provider.''

"That good old man,'' said Molly. "How I love him. When I heard what he had done to save McTee . . . that was what first showed me that McTee was a good man at heart.''

"Humph,'' said the unemotional sheriff.

"But have you seen him at Donnelly's?''

"From a distance.''

"Then you knew he was going there all this time and could have taken him any time you wanted . . . ?''

"I could have got myself shot up by a young fighting demon,'' said the sheriff, but nevertheless he smiled. "I didn't want to take him until I had to. Now I have to. The only thing that can save him is for him to run away. And the only thing between heaven and hell that can make him run away is you, Molly.''

"What am I to do?''

"It's pretty simple. Go elope with him, Molly. Go on up

230

there to Donnelly's and grab your man and take him away with you."

"Sheriff . . . ," she cried, and turned scarlet. "Besides," she added, "I never could."

"You will, though," said the sheriff patiently.

"But we've only really talked that once."

"Bah," said the sheriff, "I knowed that I loved my wife before I'd ever heard her speak a word. Look here, I'm doing a mighty illegal thing, getting a man married instead of arrested. And I got no more time to waste. I got to get back to a man-eating posse that's looking for some action tonight. Get into the saddle and ride for Donnelly's, Molly. You can make a good man out of that damned fool. Go ahead and do it!"

That was the last fight of Safety McTee. He was taken in hand, so to speak, and transported over the hills to a distant range, and on that range he was settled in a small ranch house. His battles thereafter were with cows and weather and prices and the other allies and enemies of cattlemen.

He had friends to fight the fight with him, however. Old Donnelly and his two sons took their scars and their labor away from the old mine and moved over to the range worked by McTee. They worked together. They grew prosperous together.

And finally the old sheriff himself came over the crest of the hills, a sagging figure on a sagging horse, and told them that he had been beaten at last. They had thrust him out of office and put in a younger and a surer shot.

At first he was not very happy.

But Molly McTee sat him down in the warmest seat nearest the fire and placed her golden-headed son upon his lank knee.

"Man alive," she said, "isn't it time for you to stop working and rest a while?"

So the sheriff began to rest.

Max Brand

"But," he said once upon a time, "did any of you ever hear before of a gent that collected happiness at the point of a gun the way Safety McTee has been doing?"

To read the work of Max Brand is to experience the Old West in all of its glory, energy, and humanity. And here, all restored to their original length, and collected in paperback for the first time, are three of Max Brand's greatest short novels. In "Winking Lights," a chance encounter and burning curiosity lead a rider to an ancient hacienda and a trapped young woman. A tenderfoot in a Mexican border town learns hard lessons about trusting gunfighters in "The Best Bandit." And in the title novel, a frontier gambler is given a rare second chance in life . . . if he's willing to take it.

___4508-7 $4.99 US/$5.99 CAN

MAX BRAND
SIXTEEN IN NOME

Joe May, an overgrown youth with a skinny neck and a large Adam's apple, has eaten only once in the last thirty-six hours and is feeling desperate. When he provides a small service for Hugh Massey, owner of the most famous husky in Alaska, all Joe has in mind is a possible reward. He heard that Massey's life revolves around that dog . . . and a chance to murder the man he hates with an undying rage. But he never thinks he will become the bait Massey needs to lure his enemy into a deadly trap—a trap that will set off an epic trek across hundreds of miles of frozen country, to a river of ice known as the Yukon.

___4486-2 $4.50 US/$5.50 CAN